MOUNT RUSHMORE, BADLANDS, WIND CAVE

Going Underground

Adventures ... Parkers

FALCONGUIDES®

FalconGuides is an imprint of Globe Pequot Press.
Falcon, FalconGuides, and Outfit Your Mind are registered trademarks of Morris Book Publishing, LLC.

Photo credits:
Licensed by Shutterstock.com: inside cover and i: © Ralf Broskvar; 1: © Lisa Woodburn; 3: © Tomaz Kunst; 18: © pzig98; 34: © Tomaz Kunst; 42 (top): © Mermozine; 44: © iofoto; 47: © George Aldridge; 48: © solpo; 52: © Ryan M. Bolton; 56: © J. Norman Reid; 72 (top): © iofoto; 72 bottom: © Jason Patrick Ross; 74: © Krzysztof Wiktoe; 82: © Krzysztof Wiktoe; 81 (top): © Elizabeth C. Doerner; 82 (top and bottom): © Jody Dingle; 91 and 93: © Jim Parkin; 94: © trekandshoot
© Mike Graf: 4; 5; 6; 9; 10; 11; 15; 16–17; 20; 22 (both); 24; 27; 28; 29; 30; 33; 37; 40 (both); 42 (bottom); 45 (both); 49; 55; 66
Courtesy National Park Service: 43; 61; 62; 69; 70; 76; 77; 87
South Dakota Office of Tourism: 81 (bottom)
Maps courtesy of National Park Service

Illustrations: Marjorie Leggitt
Models for twins: Amanda and Ben Frazier

Project editor: David Legere

Library of Congress Cataloging-in-Publication Data is available on file.

ISBN 978-0-7627-7968-0

Printed in the United States of America
10 9 8 7 6 5 4 3 2 1

The Saber-Toothed Hunter

One Day, Thirty-three Million Years Ago

A small body of water was nestled within the grassy plain. Tall hackberry trees surrounded the watering hole, the only one for miles around. It had not rained for quite some time. The prehistoric region was under a severe drought.

The sun baked down and the whole area warmed, sweltering under the intense heat hanging in the air. A tortoise lying on a rock stuck its head up. But the midday sun was just too warm. The tortoise tucked its head back in while staying perched on the boulder in the middle of the isolated watering hole.

Nearby, a herd of Mesohippus, *prehistoric miniature horses, grazed on the leaves of the ferns surrounding the lake. The height of a modern fox, the creatures tore off shreds of the plant and ground them with their flat teeth into a chewy pulp.*

A large piglike creature with a four-foot-long head trotted up. The Archaeotherium *bent down and lapped up some water, then lumbered off, stopping to rest in the shade of a palm tree.*

Nearby, a Subhyracodon *was also staying close to the watering hole. The hornless ancient rhino wallowed in the muck near the shoreline, getting deeper in the mud with every step.*

A moment later a nearly starving saber-toothed cat ran up. The powerful predator lapped up some water, then scoured the vicinity, searching for prey. The beast took a few steps toward the herd of Mesohippus, *then stopped in the shade behind a bushy fern and waited where it was a little cooler. A few moments later, the cat began to stalk one of the smaller* Mesohippus.

The fox-sized prehistoric horse caught a glimpse of the approaching predator. It glanced back, then ran straight toward the water.

The saber-toothed cat watched the creature swim toward the middle of the water hole. The Mesohippus *bleated loudly as its head bobbed and weaved above the surface.*

The saber-toothed cat paced back and forth, then rambled across the shallow water and started paddling after the struggling Mesohippus. *Soon the* Mesohippus *stepped into deep mud at the bottom of the watering hole.*

The large cat reached the trapped animal. It snarled and dove toward the stuck, panicking creature. The cat swatted at its side, striking the small herbivore across the face, and the Mesohippus *screeched in distress. The cat*

then lunged onto the Mesohippus's *neck, clamping onto and tearing into the creature right at the base of its skull and through the jaw.*

Both mammals rolled and struggled in the water, simultaneously dipping under the surface before coming up for air.

A few moments later the battling creatures submerged again, only this time not to re-surface. And soon, it became calm; all prehistoric beasts were now out of sight.

Both the Mesohippus *and the saber-toothed cat were now drowned at the bottom of the thick, muddy water hole. Over time, other prehistoric animals in the vicinity met similar fates.*

Buried

As drought continued to parch the region, several perished animals lay on the former watering hole's dry, mud-caked bottom. Then silt and ash layered onto the once ferocious beasts. The prehistoric mammals were now buried under piling sediment.

Over time, the area became cooler and drier, although periodic floods covered the region, depositing layers of sand, silt, and ash. The buried beasts were all far below the ground, and all that was left of them were bones and teeth—their skin and flesh had long since rotted away.

Then something peculiar began to happen. Gradually the once-living material in the animals was replaced, one microscopic speck at a time, by minerals seeping through the surrounding rock. Bit by bit and over millions of years the bones and teeth were all transforming into a rock- and mineral-laden cast replica of their former selves. And yet these fossils remained beneath the massive layers of sediment.

Streams ran fast through the region, cutting into the easily eroded conglomeration of soils in the area.

Then about five hundred thousand years ago, most of the nearby streams were channeled into the Cheyenne River. This caused the Badlands area to be starved of sediment, which greatly increased erosion in the area.

Around ten thousand years ago a cool, wet period of time accelerated this process. Rivers of water washed through the region, eroding away the softer, malleable soil layers into fantastic, bizarre shapes.

Meanwhile the prehistoric bones buried deep below inched closer and closer to the surface with each passing storm and period of intense erosion.

Suddenly, around 1843, fur trappers discovered the first bones sticking up out of Badlands' sediments and researchers wrote a publication about them in 1846. The modern era of scientific discovery had begun here, and it would lead to the Badlands becoming one of the richest prehistoric fossilized mammal regions in the world.

And this all leads us up to the summer when Robert and Kristen Parker and their ten-year-old twins, Morgan and James, decided to take a trip to this spectacular region of national parks.

Welcome to the Badlands

In the Modern World

The Parkers arrived at Badlands driving from the west on Highway 44. They moved slowly through the tiny town of Interior and then entered the park. The family gazed out the window at the sea of wind-waving grasses in the foreground and the barren, eroded buttes in the distance. Mom commented, "It's so different here than any national park I've ever seen—a grassland prairie with a bunch of bizzarely shaped badlands."

The Parkers pulled into the campground and quickly set up their tent and paid for their site. Then, with much of the afternoon still ahead, they drove toward the heart of the park and several short trails.

The road took the family past Cedar Pass Lodge and the visitor center. "We'll go there later," Dad remarked.

Dad drove slowly up Cedar Pass and toward a convoluted maze of badlands. As they approached the top, the family stared at the close-up views of the highly unusual scenery.

"Badlands," Dad called out in awe, "sure are amazing!"

"And photogenic," Morgan added while snapping a few pictures through the rolled-down window.

Before long the family arrived at a parking lot. Dad pulled in and they all piled out.

"Well—let's go!" James exclaimed with enthusiasm at a trailhead. But a few feet later he stopped with alarm. "Look at this sign!" he pointed.

Straight ahead a warning was posted for all hikers: BEWARE OF RATTLESNAKES!

"Hmm," Mom pondered. "We'll have to be extra careful where we step out here."

The Parkers walked along the short Cliff Shelf Nature Trail. The half-mile-long walkway was a combination of gravel and boardwalk with sets of stairs. At the top of the trail the family paused to gaze out at the vista. From there they could see the lodge and campground nestled in the distant prairie.

"That's where we're staying!" Morgan exclaimed.

As the family admired the views, a series of vans, trucks, and cars all pulled into the lodge's parking lot. After the caravan of vehicles parked, Dad said, "I wonder what's going on down there."

Meanwhile Morgan scanned the skies as well as the buttes and badlands looking for a good angle for a picture. She took several of the scenery, but also a few of a massive, billowing thunderstorm.

"Look at that cloud!" Morgan exclaimed. "It has bulges at its bottom that look like pillows."

"Good description," Dad said. "Those are mammatus clouds at the base of a building thunderstorm. We're in the Great Plains now. And these conditions are much more common here this time of year than where we're from in California." Dad studied the blossoming cloud with a dark grey base for a moment longer, trying to decipher the direction it was moving. "I think we'll be fine on this little trail, at least for the short term."

Storm's coming

The Parkers plowed on. The path dropped into a small juniper forest before looping back to the trailhead. Then the family drove to the Door and Window Trails, just up the road.

A large group of cars was parked there. The Parkers checked the sky again and determined the developing thunderstorm was not heading their way at that moment. Then the family proceeded down the short path called the Window Trail.

The walkway soon ended at a railing overlooking the badlands. The family stood there, gazing into a spectacularly eroded canyon sculpted out of dirt and clay. "Wow!" Dad exclaimed. "I can really see how water washes through there and carves up the gully."

Next the family crossed the parking lot over to the Door Trail. Another boardwalk led the family to a small set of stairs. From there the Parkers gazed into the heart of the convoluted, eroded scenery.

A sign below the stairs proclaimed that the area was the "baddest" of all the badlands, beckoning hikers to go out and explore. The Parkers ventured a ways beyond the sign, following a series of small posts planted into the ground leading into the sparsely vegetated wilderness.

BADDEST OF THE BADLANDS

In some places on earth, soft, highly erodable clays are the dominant sediment type. These sediments are sculpted by wind, rain, and frost over time into spectacular and bizarrely shaped canyons, gullies, ravines, and other odd geologic formations. Many badlands are also uniquely colored due to the mineral contents in the clay soil, and such is the case at Badlands National Park.

At one point, James gazed into a deeply eroded chasm. "I sure wouldn't want to get stuck in one of those!" he remarked.

The family's concern over the threatening sky put an end to their journey. But, as they were returning to their car, sun peeked back through and beckoned them on. They decided to hike the last trail of the area, the Notch Trail.

This time the path started by heading up a dirt gully. "Now we're hiking!" Dad announced with a satisfied sigh.

Ladder on the Notch Trail

A short while later the dirt trail turned a corner. Straight ahead a ladder was perched onto a bluff. Morgan gauged the situation. "I guess we're climbing!"

Morgan and James took the lead, walking briskly toward the steeply positioned ladder. They got to the base of the bluff and waited for their parents to catch up. Once Mom and Dad were there, the twins looked at them, asking without saying a word.

"Go ahead," Mom said.

"Yeah, we'll watch you so we can see where the tough parts are," Dad added.

First Morgan, then James zipped up the ladder. Near the top the pitch steepened but the twins easily reached the blufftop, stepped off the ladder, and then turned to gaze down at their parents.

"Come on!" James called down. "It's not that hard."

Once they were all reunited, Dad brushed himself off and said, "Well, that was a little adventure!"

The family continued on, passing a sign warning hikers to stay away from the cliff edge. The trail now traversed among the bluffs and buttes. Mom took the lead, guiding her family along the narrow path while making sure the footing was secure. Finally they came to two signposts with arrows both pointing toward the right. "I guess that's the way," James said.

The Parkers scrambled up the last section of the "Notch." Once at the top they peeked over the other side. Morgan was first to notice a distinct path almost directly below them. "Hey! That's where we were earlier," she called out.

"It's the Cliff Shelf Trail," Mom realized.

"And our campground way out there," James added, gazing into the distance.

Meanwhile, Dad again inspected the skies. A towering, dark cumulonimbus cloud was to the south, but its expanding mass now blocked the sun where the Parkers stood. In the distance, the base of the cloud had white shafts of precipitation dropping below it. Right in that location a rogue lightning bolt lit up underneath the cloud, appearing to strike the ground.

"Did you guys see that?" Morgan exclaimed.

"Sure did," Dad replied. "Tornado Alley can really put on a show with thunderstorms."

After a moment, Dad continued, "but the brunt of the storm seems pretty far off. There wasn't any thunder."

Still, Dad studied the unusual, circular formation at the bottom of the cloud. "Wow," he said, "the whole base of the cloud appears to be rotating!"

Morgan, James, and Mom also looked up. "What do you mean?" James asked.

"Sometimes thunderstorms out here become supercells. They take on a mind of their own and rotate in a large circular pattern. Rotation is an indication that the storm might become or already is tornadic."

"Is that what you meant by Tornado Alley?" Morgan asked.

"Yep," Dad said. "A perfect blend of tornado-producing atmospheric conditions brews in these Midwestern states from March until June every year."

"It's June 27," Mom added. "It's still tornado season, then."

The family watched the thunderstorm from their vantage point, wondering if they were going to see a funnel cloud spin down. But only sheets of rain and hail appeared below the giant cloud's base. Still, the cloud swelled before their eyes, further darkening the skies. The wind picked up and it became noticeably cooler. A few drops of heat-breaking rain plunked down around the Parkers.

At the same time shafts of sunlight and shade gave the views of the badlands an ethereal, vibrant quality. Morgan snapped several pictures.

Suddenly a bolt of lightning flashed and distant thunder followed. Mom snapped to. "We better go," she announced.

The Parkers turned around to leave, but as they scampered back to the signposts, two large animals blocked their path.

"Whoa!" Mom said, putting the brakes on her family.

Two bighorn sheep were right on the trail. The mother glanced at the Parkers. Then she nuzzled her baby.

"Sorry. We didn't mean to disturb you," Mom whispered to the noble-looking animals.

The mother nudged her baby again and this time the animals took off and quickly scrambled up a butte.

"I wish I could climb like that," James said in awe.

The family returned to the ladder, climbed down, and finished the walk in the gully. More large drops of rain splatted down. An occasional flash of lightning reminded the Parkers that it was time to head indoors.

By the time Morgan, James, Mom, and Dad returned to the parking lot, a full-blown thunderstorm burst forth. The Parkers sprinted toward their car. Now, tiny balls of ice—hail—accompanied the sheets of rain blowing across the blacktop.

Mom pulled out the car key as she ran. She pushed a button, opening the doors before they got there. The Parkers quickly piled in, shut the doors, and laughed, noticing each other's wet mops of hair.

"Well, that was fun!" Dad said. Then he shook his head, showering his family with secondhand raindrops.

Wind and rain continued to pummel the landscape. The family waited a moment, then Mom checked the time. "Three twenty," she announced. "Maybe it's not the best time for that fossil talk in ten minutes."

"We can always try it again tomorrow morning at ten thirty," Dad said. "They offer it twice a day."

And with that the Parkers drove toward the visitor center and lodge. They opted for the lodge first. Once they got there, the series of trucks, cars, and vans the family had glimpsed earlier were still parked in front. Several had unusual logos on them: STORM SAFARI and LIGHTNING CHASER were two of them. Others were also adorned with images of tornadoes, lightning, and massive clouds.

"Well," Dad said, inspecting the vehicles. "It looks like we have some interesting company inside!"

Hanging Out with Chasers

The rebuilding thunderstorm chased the Parkers from their car into the lodge. At the entrance a small sign greeted them. DESIGNATED STORM SHELTER, it read, with a picture of a tornado.

Inside, a gift shop was to the left and a cashier for the hotel registry was straight ahead. But the buzz of activity appeared to be coming from the cafe to the right.

The Parkers heard all the commotion in the restaurant and wandered over. They were greeted by a hostess with four menus. "Would you like to sit down?" she asked.

Dad held up his hand. "Hang on a second," he responded.

The cafe was packed with groups of people poring over maps, studying computer screens, and talking on cell phones. With all of the activity going on, the Parkers couldn't pick out much of what was being discussed.

Dad took a step closer and leaned into the small restaurant. He was able to hear bits of conversation. Then Dad turned toward his family. "They're all talking about the severe thunderstorm," he reported.

Now all four Parkers edged closer. "Someone just mentioned a tornado touching down," James exclaimed.

Morgan caught more tidbits. "It was about twenty miles away from here."

Mom noticed a table next to one of the groups had just opened up. As a waiter cleaned it, Mom turned toward the hostess. "Can we sit over there?"

"Sure. It'll be just a minute before we can finish cleaning it up."

Then Mom looked at her family. "Does an early dinner sound all right?"

"I don't think we'll be able to cook outside with this weather anyway," Dad replied.

"Outside," Morgan repeated, thinking of the night ahead. "At least our tent is set up!"

Mom and Dad paused while walking toward the table. Then Dad said, "We'll see what condition it's in when we get there."

The Parkers sat down. As they did, James looked out the window. At that moment, the storm seemed to be letting up—and shafts of sunlight poked between the clouds. Then, while perusing the menu, Morgan, James, Mom, and Dad eavesdropped on the animated conversations surrounding them.

"Pretty active today," one storm chaser said at a nearby table.

"We did have a few, brief funnel clouds and that small tornado. Good thing there was no serious damage. Just some downed trees and a shed roof was torn off. But tomorrow our whole caravan hits the road."

"The atmospheric ingredients are brewing for major action east of Rapid City."

Soon the Parkers ordered their early supper. While waiting they continued listening in on the meteorologists and others with them. One was poring over a map. He also had his computer on in front of him. "Good thing they have wireless Internet here," he announced while studying the radar loop on the computer.

Then he noticed the Parkers were staring at his computer screen. "Look," he said, turning the monitor so Morgan, James, Mom, and Dad could get a better view. It showed a satellite and radar combination loop. "That supercell really exploded this afternoon. And here's the small hook-echo where the tornado touched down. But it's all starting to dissipate, at least for right now."

Dad wanted to know more and asked, "So I take it all of you are meteorologists, storm chasers pursuing the severe weather?"

A woman in the group spoke up. "We're not all meteorologists, but we are all out doing our favorite thing—chasing severe storms," she explained enthusiastically. "Some of us, like my husband and I, are on vacation doing this. Others are the weather experts taking us along for the ride."

The nearby group introduced themselves to the Parkers and Mom introduced her family back.

James asked, "You're really on vacation doing this?"

"Yes. We're on a Storm Chaser Safari. They're offered every year here on the plains from March until June in prime tornado season. This one guarantees close-up severe weather spotting. And so far they've been right on."

Dad peeked again at the latest radar loop playing on the computer. "It was quite a storm we had a little while ago."

"Yes, but it was mostly just rain here. To the south they got hit worse. The tornado apparently touched down where there were no roads so we couldn't get anywhere near it. Here at Badlands National Park, the rain produced some muddy, swollen streams but that's about all."

At the front of the cafe a park ranger walked in. He said hello to the hostess, then walked over to several of the chasers gathered at a table.

"Well, so much for my fossil talk," he announced.

"What happened?" one of the chasers asked.

"I had to cancel it, although I first tried to continue on inside the shelter out there. But there was just too much weather going on. Lightning. Rain. Hail. We had it all. It was too distracting, and dangerous as well. So I sent everyone quickly back to their vehicles when there was a little break in the action. Right after that the real downpour hit!" The ranger added, "But, really, thanks for bringing the crazy weather with you!"

The group of storm chasers looked at the ranger, waiting for an explanation. Then he changed the topic from meteorology to paleontology.

"We needed the rain. It's been so dry out here, almost to the point of a drought, but, more than that, storms like the one we just had are great news for the park's paleontologists. The erosion really increases with the flash floods and that ups their chances of finding any fossils exposed on the surface of the soil."

The ranger said good-bye to the storm chasers and wandered out of the restaurant.

Meanwhile, the Parkers finished their dinner. Afterwards, when they walked outside, the skies had partially cleared. Only broken clouds dotted the horizon. "Well," Mom said, "Let's go check out the damage in camp."

It was just after 6 p.m. and the parking lot was full of ponds making for little watering holes for the local birds and rabbits. "I wonder if the tent is soaked," James said.

"Or if it's even standing," Morgan added, recalling all the wind that had accompanied the storm.

The Parkers drove to the nearby campground. They found their site, and their tent was tipped sideways and blown about twenty feet away from where they had staked it. They turned it upright, shook off the excess water, and restaked it at their site, then checked the inside. "At least our bedding wasn't in there, so we'll be dry enough tonight!" Mom announced.

Early Morning Hikers?

At the crack of dawn the Parkers got up quickly and readied for their hike into the heart of the Badlands. By 6:30 a.m. they were on the road to the Saddle Pass Trailhead.

Once there, Mom parked the car in the empty parking lot. The family threw snacks and water into their packs and began the short but steep journey up Saddle Pass.

Saddle Pass Trailhead

The morning was mostly clear and the air cool and moist after the thunderstorms of the day before. Morgan, James, Mom, and Dad stepped down a slope and hopped over a small muddy stream.

As they followed signposts indicating the trail, mud began collecting on their shoes with each step. A short stretch later the flat trail shifted to one up a steep slope toward the top of the pass and the buttes and badlands above.

The Parkers tromped along, their steps becoming heavy with thick, clinging mud. At one point, James stopped and began scraping the bottom of his shoe against a rock. But as he did he slowly started sliding down the trail. "Whoa!" James exclaimed while balancing himself like a surfer on a board.

A few feet later James bumped into Dad and then placed his foot against his father's, ending his slow-motion downhill journey. James smiled and looked at his family. "That was kind of fun!"

From there, the Parkers carefully continued up the steepening trail. At times the whole family had to get on all fours just to keep from sliding back.

On a slightly more level spot, Dad dashed upward but slipped right into the mud. Then he called down. "Let me try again and just get to that rock up there." Without any hesitation, Dad sprint-crawled up the steep section. He made it about twenty feet farther and braced himself against the rock. He quickly scraped some mud off his hands and turned around. "Okay, everyone, go one at a time and I'll grab you when you get close."

Morgan scampered toward Dad. She slid backward on some steps and held her ground on others. Still, somehow, she managed to make it close enough to Dad until he grabbed her hand and yanked Morgan up the remaining distance. Then Dad pointed just above him. "Can you plant your foot on that rock and wait there?" Morgan did so.

James and Mom followed Morgan's footsteps up the hill. Soon the Parkers were beyond the steepest and muddiest sections of trail. A short while later they were finally at the top of the pass. Each found rocks to scrape the mud off their shoes and hands, at least as much as they could.

The family proceeded to the junction of the Medicine Root and Castle Trails. James glanced at the sign, and at the park map. "This way!" he announced with enthusiasm. And with that the Parkers were hiking on the Medicine Root Trail.

A second later, though, they stopped. Another rattlesnake warning sign stood ominously next to the path. Mom stepped to the front. "Follow me!" she said. "I'll keep a look out. Morning's an active time for snakes."

The mostly flat pathway weaved its way among the wild prairie grasslands of Badlands National Park. The tall blowing grasses were sprinkled with drops of water from the recent rain. Birds flitted about while others perched on top of the small, eroded stacks or buttes. Wildflowers adorned the trail and an occasional prickly pear cactus grew right next to the worn walkway.

Badlands grasses

At times the trail was hard to pick out—lost among the tall

grasses. The family had to stop at several points to decipher where the next signpost was indicating the path.

At other spots the landscape opened up and the trail was rocky and near small washes that had eroded downward like mini canyons. In the distance the buttes, pyramids, and pinnacles of the Badlands adorned the horizon.

One part of the trail had small muddy puddles on it. Mom started to walk around the small water holes until Morgan, right behind her, called out, "Wait! Stop!"

Mom obeyed Morgan's command then Morgan pointed out part of an object protruding from the mud. Dad saw it too, and whispered, "Good eyes, Morgan!"

A fist-sized, pale-colored toad breathed in, swelling its neck and belly. Then the amphibian exhaled and shrank, apparently unaware that it was being observed.

But it wasn't just the Parkers watching it. James noticed the other animal first. "Look!" he exclaimed.

A large, thick, yellow-banded snake was slowly slithering its way out of the grass. It flicked its tongue in and out of its mouth and glided toward the toad.

Mom guided her family back a few steps. "Is it a rattlesnake?" Morgan whispered.

"No," Mom replied. "I think it's a bull snake. And they are known to have a nasty temperament and painful bite."

The Parkers watched the reptile creep closer to its prey. Then, in one fell swoop, it struck the toad, clamping down on the amphibian, and then opening its jaws, it began using its muscles to slowly inhale the whole creature.

Morgan, James, Mom, and Dad watched the proceedings. At first the toad kicked and struggled while its legs stuck out of the snake's mouth. But once the toad was mostly inside it apparently died, and swallowing was now smoother for the snake. Soon the toad was out of sight altogether and the only evidence of it was a large lump in the snake's throat. At that point the bull snake retreated into the grass and disappeared. The Parkers hurriedly scampered by, then James turned toward his family, grinning. "You don't get to see that every day!"

The family cruised on, passing more grasslands and an occasional, isolated butte of rock. Soon they came to the Castle Trail. At the junction of the two paths, Dad pulled out some trail mix and took out a small handful. "Anyone else?" he asked.

James shook his head no, and pulled out his map. He pointed toward the Castle Trail, "I think we go that way now."

Mom looked over James's shoulder. "Hey, there's a road up there," she realized. "I thought this area was all just trails. I'm surprised. I want to go up there and check it out."

Mom began walking and Morgan and James followed. Meanwhile Dad was staring off toward an isolated butte with a small bird on top. He studied the bird, then pulled out the binoculars for a closer look. "I'll wait here," Dad said. "You all go on ahead."

As Morgan, Mom, and James got closer to the road they noticed a parked car. Mom looked up and saw two men at the car scurrying about with equipment. Mom stopped behind a patch of tall grass and held out her arms to the twins. "Hang on a second," she said.

Morgan, James, and Mom remained hidden behind the grass while they watched the two men in muddy clothes hurriedly throw rock hammers and packs into the back of the car. They slammed the hatch shut, and then dashed into the car.

The driver, wearing a red cap, started the engine, while his companion tossed more gear into the back, and then laughed mischievously. The guy in the red cap gave his friend a high five and then accelerated the car and drove away quickly, leaving behind a trail of dust.

Once the vehicle was out of sight, Mom took a deep breath. "Well, that was a bit unnerving."

"What do you think they were doing?" Morgan asked.

"Whatever it was they got up pretty early to do it," Mom remarked, referring to the time of day.

"And did you see those buckets of rocks in the back?" James mentioned.

"Rocks?" Mom said nervously. "I was studying their faces. Are you sure that's what you saw?"

445 ALX

"Yes," James replied. "They had at least three or four buckets full of rocks in the back."

"Come on," Mom said. And they hustled back to Dad.

Once they were back to the trail junction, Mom grabbed the map, then took a pen from her pack and jotted some things down.

"What are you doing?" Dad asked.

"Something weird just happened," Mom replied. And Mom, James, and Morgan told Dad about the car and the two men's unusual behavior. Then Mom added, "Whatever they were up to doesn't seem right. I just wrote down their license plate and color and make of their car. I think we should report what happened as soon as we can to a ranger."

"Good eyes!" Morgan said.

Dad looked back at the sign indicating the Castle Trail. "Come on," he said to his family. "I'm also thinking we shouldn't be hanging around here anymore."

The often barren Badlands

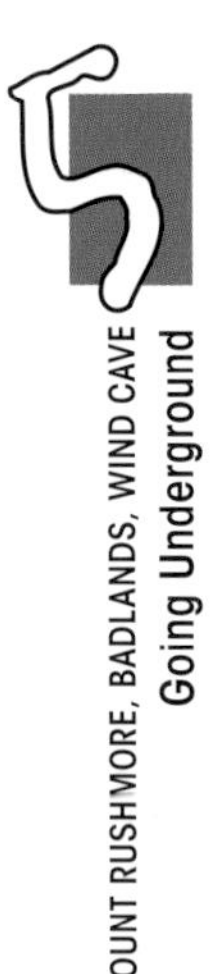

An Amazing Discovery

The Parkers continued on the backcountry loop, which now wandered over to the buttes, pinnacles, and bluffs and the heart of the erosional scenery. The family, at first, moved briskly along, wanting to get some distance between themselves and the odd event that had just occurred at the trail junction.

Soon they passed a couple of other early-morning hikers. After that the family was a bit more at ease. Morgan, James, Mom, and Dad slowed down a little and they began to admire the lunar-like barren bluffs paralleling the trail.

At one point a large shiny black beetle scampered along the path. The Parkers briefly stopped to watch the insect scoot by. Then they carefully stepped over it and continued walking.

Eventually they returned to the junction above Saddle Pass. "Well," Mom said. "That sure was an interesting morning."

Dad gazed ahead, quietly pondering. "You know," he said, "your journey among these castles of dirt and rock doesn't have to end just yet."

Morgan, James, and Mom looked at Dad, waiting for an explanation. So Dad shared his idea.

"We must have walked really fast because it's still early, only nine a.m.," he said, "and the fossil talk is at ten thirty. What I'm thinking is that all of us don't really need to go down that muddy pass. It's so thick and slippery, and probably not even completely safe. What we could do instead," Dad suggested, "is I'll go down Saddle Pass and get the car. The three of you can hike the last two miles along the Castle Trail and we'll all meet at the fossil talk parking lot where the trail comes out in plenty of time for the ranger presentation. And we can tell the ranger there about the incident we saw today on the trail."

James pulled out the park map and the family looked it over, considering Dad's idea.

"I think it's a perfect plan," Mom replied.

"Deal or no deal?" Dad said, waiting for the final decision.

"Deal!" Morgan and James announced in unison, while Mom nodded in agreement.

And with that the Parkers split up, Morgan, James, and

Rock castles

Mom hiking along the last section of the Castle Trail and Dad heading down the pass.

The Castle Trail continued to wander among the buttes, bluffs, and pinnacles. Morgan stopped to take several photos while James and Mom took occasional side treks to peek into gullies and washes and examine the erosional features. The mostly flat trail seemed even more remote, but the relative isolation was offset by the bright morning sun, and the fact that they were less than two miles to Dad and the parking area.

Along the Castle Trail

Meanwhile, Dad worked his way down Saddle Pass. The top, steep part was drier than earlier in the day, but some sections were still quite slick. At one spot, Dad just let his feet glide down, leaving a skid mark in his wake. "I hate messing up the trail like that," Dad said to no one in particular, "But, hopefully, later, the footprints of other hikers or more rain will cover up my tracks."

Dad managed to scamper down the steeper sections and worked his way toward flatter ground. As he approached the car he began shuffling his feet along the path, removing as much mud as he could while he walked. When Dad reached the parking area he spent several minutes scraping his shoes off on the pavement. When the weight of his step seemed closer to normal, Dad scraped off a little more and got in the car and drove to the Fossil Exhibit area. There Dad parked the car and glanced at the nearly empty parking lot. He checked his watch: 9:40 a.m. Then Dad began walking toward his family on the Castle Trail.

Meanwhile, Morgan, James, and Mom continued to meander along. With less than a mile left and over half an hour to go they began to slow down. The three Parkers continued to admire the scenery and occasionally went off path to check out gullies and washes. They were doing exactly that when, about fifty feet away from the trail, James saw something unusual sticking out of the ground.

"Hey, you guys!" James called out with nervous anticipation.

Morgan and Mom jogged over to the gully for an inspection. Mom kneeled down for a closer look. Then she stood up and touched her chin. "Wow!" she exclaimed. "That is definitely not a rock."

"You mean it's a bone?" James replied, excitedly.

"My guess is a leg bone," Mom said. She looked again and pointed it out to the twins. "You can see a bonelike pattern and texture in it, although it's been fossilized into a rock over the eons. Also, there appears to be some symmetry—one side mirrors the other. That doesn't happen with rocks."

"So it's a fossil, then?" Morgan asked to make sure.

"Yes," Mom replied. "The bone is also stained dark with minerals. If it was a new bone from a bison or coyote it would still be white."

"Wait a minute!" James exclaimed. "Look over here!"

Off to the side, a tangle of bonelike fossils was webbed together by the clay soils and rock. Morgan, James, and Mom inspected that area. "Unbelievable," Mom said in a hushed, reverent tone.

"So, these are all from dinosaurs?" James asked, awed by their discovery.

"Not dinosaurs," Mom replied, "because as I understand it, the Badlands area was under water during the age of the dinosaurs over sixty-five million years ago. Most likely it's fossilized mammals from about thirty-three million years ago."

"Wow!" Morgan exclaimed. "Should we dig one of the bones up, to get a better look at it?"

"No, leave them there," Mom replied. "We're supposed to report any fossils and leave them exactly where they were found."

Then a new, deeper voice spoke. "It looks like you just stumbled upon the motherlode!"

Morgan and James jumped, hearing an intruder, but calmed instantly, once they realized it was just their dad.

The family began scouring the area nearby, looking for any more fossilized remains. But after a quick search of the immediate vicinity, they only found the one spot, laden with bones on top of bones, partially sticking out of the side and on top of the small gully.

"You know," Mom realized, "without yesterday's rains we might never have had the chance to discover this."

James glanced back to the trail, about fifty feet away. "Even today we might have just walked right by it," he concluded.

"What do we do now?" Morgan asked.

"Take a bunch of pictures," Dad replied to Morgan. "Go for it. Take them of the bones and the whole area where you found them."

Then Mom turned to James. "Can you pull out the map?"

James did so and he and Mom guesstimated their location on the Castle Trail and marked an X on that spot on the map. Then Mom said, "James, do you mind writing some notes down about some of the features in the area? We need to report to the rangers exactly where we found this."

Dad chimed in. "Write down what parts of the body we think those bones are, too." Dad paused and looked at Mom. "What do you think?"

"It's hard to be certain about all of them without digging. But I'm pretty sure there are at least parts of vertebrae and limbs, and maybe some ribs, too. We need an expert out here." Mom looked up at her family, beaming. "It's a whole bed of bones, though!"

James wrote the possible bone types down in his notes.

The Parkers' thorough documentation of their discovery took quite some time, delaying their hike out on the Castle Trail. By the time they left the site it was about 10:30 a.m., the time of the fossil talk. Morgan, James, Mom, and Dad hustled along on the last section of trail.

As they walked, Morgan mentioned, "There's no way I'll ever not be able to find that site."

"That's good," Mom said, "because we might have to."

And James added. "Now we have two things to report to the ranger."

At almost a quarter to eleven, the Parkers arrived at the trailhead parking lot. The family crossed the street and hustled over to a large group of people gathered at a shelter. "Boy," Dad said, "it sure got busy around here!"

The family found a spot at the back of the group and listened to the ranger, Eric, give his presentation.

Fossil talk

Incident Reports One and Two

The Parkers pressed further into the crowded gazebo area and inched closer to the ranger, whom they recognized from the cafe.

"So," Eric went on, "a fossil is any evidence of a past animal or plant preserved in soil or rock. It might be an imprint or a footprint, not necessarily the organism itself. Or it could be actual replacement of bones, teeth, or skin."

"Replicas?" someone in the group asked.

"Yes," Eric replied. "Let me explain. Fossils can be formed by several different methods. But the primary process is permineralization. And this is the only one we'll focus on today."

PRESERVING THE PAST

Fossils can include molds where an impression of the organism is preserved in the ground or a hole. Cast fossils occur when that hole is filled in with soils and minerals and still retains the shape of the organism. Trace fossils are fossilized nests, burrows, and footprints, but not the animal part itself. True fossils are formed by the actual animal or part of the animal.

"Permineralization is the replacement of the original organic matter, or living tissue, with material from the surrounding rock. It works like this. An animal dies and sinks to the bottom of a lake, pond, or stream, or

any body of water. This is important because to be preserved in the soil, it must be buried at least within a fairly recent time period after its death.

"Scavengers such as microorganisms and insects devour the tissues before they are buried in sand, silt, or, as it was around here, volcanic ash. Soil layers keep building, making a protective barrier from any further damage that can be inflicted on the animal's remains. More and more sediments build up over time.

"And that's when permineralization starts. As the animal's skeleton decays, mineral-laden water passes through, replacing the bone with rocklike minerals. Eventually the whole skeleton (or teeth or bones) is now a rocklike replica of its original self. The fossil resembles the original creature, but it's really sedimentary rock. All of its original color is also gone.

"Then sun, wind, rain, and ice start to erode or wash away the rock layers, bringing the fossil closer and closer to the surface.

"And that's where paleontology comes into play! And I've got a few of our fossil friends right in here."

Eric reached into a box and pulled out a fossil. "This leg bone," he held the fossil up, "is part of a *Mesohippus*. It was a three-toed horse that lived around here. We know of their horse ancestry because their teeth and limb structure resemble today's horses."

Eric pulled out another. "This is part of the jaw of a *Subhyracodon*. It also lived in this region. It was a plant eater considered to be an early rhino, related to today's rhinos by its teeth."

"And finally," Eric grabbed another ancient bone from the box. "This creature was a saber-toothed cat." The ranger showed a partial jaw. "The saber-tooth lived in the vicinity although its fossil is rarely found—we only have a few remains of the saber-tooth. There were also different species of the cat and they ranged in size from a bobcat to a small mountain lion. They were fast runners and sprang upon their prey."

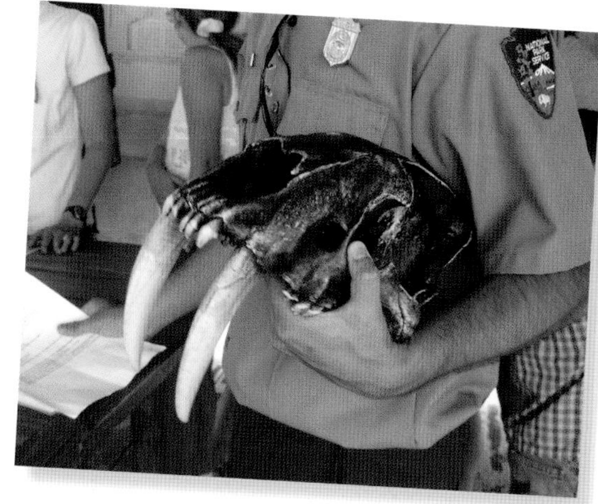

"So," Eric built to his conclusion. "Badlands fossils are a window into the past. And we never know where they'll resurface. In the early 1990s two fellows from Iowa found a fossilized backbone near the Conata Picnic area. They reported it as they should have on a form like this."

All four Parkers inched closer and gazed at the paper Eric held up. Then they glanced at each other in anticipation.

"We thought it would take just a few days to dig up the fossils in that area. But, fifteen years and nineteen thousand fossils later, the dig finally concluded!"

"And by the way, paleontologists like to go out searching after rains like we had yesterday. A little erosion can go a long way to helping find some ancient bones!"

James and Morgan looked at each other, smiling.

"Consider walking out on the short Fossil Exhibit Trail to see some cast replicas of what we've found out here . . . and enjoy your stay in the Badlands."

The group clapped for Eric. He stood around and answered some questions while many of the visitors inspected the fossils he brought along.

Meanwhile, as people slowly left, Morgan, James, Mom, and Dad urgently inched their way closer to the front. Once they got there, they patiently looked over the fossils and waited for Eric to finish chatting with some of the other visitors.

Finally, Morgan took another quick step toward Eric and the family followed. Morgan glanced at Mom and Dad. "Go ahead," Mom said. "Tell him."

Morgan took a deep breath and said, "We saw something wrong going on near the junction of the Castle and Medicine Root Trails."

"You mean the dirt road area?"

"Yep," Morgan replied.

"What did you see?"

"It was real early this morning when we were there. Two guys were loading rock hammers and packs into their car, and other supplies. Also, my twin brother," Morgan pointed toward James, "saw buckets of rock they had in the back before they closed it."

Eric clenched his jaw. He took a deep breath, swallowed, and said, "You're certain you saw all this?"

"Yes," Mom stepped up. "And the two guys were acting sneaky about getting out of there. That's why I wrote down their license plate and car type." Mom held up a piece of paper with the information.

"Okay," Eric said, grabbing the paper. "Hang on a second."

Eric got out his hand radio. He called in to park dispatch all the information from the Parkers, and they relayed back that the suspect party wasn't permitted to be out there on a dig and that a law enforcement patrol was going to be sent out to scour the area. Officers were also going to be notified and given the make of the car.

When Eric got off the radio, he explained to the Parkers, "You did the right thing by reporting this. It sounds like some people were out poaching bones this morning and that definitely is a problem out here. That car was not registered to be on any paleontological dig. Thank you for letting us know!"

Then James stepped forward. "I think we also need one of those papers," he pointed.

"A site report form?" Eric handed one to James. "Was there something else you saw?"

James told Eric about the bones he and his family stumbled upon near the Castle Trail.

Eric listened intently. Finally, when James finished, Eric said, "Boy you sure had quite a hike this morning."

Morgan stepped up with her camera. "We have pictures! Do you want to see?"

"I'd love to see them."

Morgan flipped through the photos of their discovery. Meanwhile, James, Mom, and Dad filled out the site report form, including marking an X on the map provided, where they thought the fossils were near the trail. They also wrote down their campsite and cell-phone numbers.

When Morgan was finished showing the photos, Eric looked up at the bright sun and pondered. He glanced at his watch. "It's approaching noon. And it's awfully hot. And as you know there's not much shade out there."

"We'd love to show you it!" James exclaimed.

Eric laughed. "Yep, you read my mind; that's what I was getting to. But, as much as I'd like to go out there and see everything, I'm not really the one you should show all this to. Badlands has a paleontologist on hand and I think she would love to check it out! I don't know about right now though. It's not the best time to be out there."

Eric looked at the Parkers. "How far off the trail would you say the fossils are?"

Morgan estimated, and then answered. "About fifty feet."

"Do you think anyone else might be able to see them?"

"I don't think so," Mom joined in. "It's in a gully and you can't see them from the trail. We just happened to wander over there."

"Well, it's not like there's going to be lots of people hiking this afternoon anyway," Eric added. "So how about we set up a time to go out there first thing in the morning. I'll check with our chief paleontologist to see if that'll work. Will you still be around?"

James answered. "Yes," and Mom and Dad concurred.

"Is seven a.m. right here at the trailhead okay? And if that doesn't work with our paleontologist, we'll leave a note at your campsite."

"Sounds great," Dad replied.

The Parkers said good-bye to Eric. They decided to take the short walk along the Fossil Exhibit Trail. Right next to the walkway on pedestals there were cast replicas of an *ammonite,* a marine invertebrate animal; *titanothere,* an alligator; *Mesohippus, Hesperocyon,* an ancient species of dogs; *nimravid,* a mammalian carnivore; and an *oreodont,* a hog-like plant eater.

Storm clouds over the Fossil Exhibit Trail

When they got to the car, Mom turned to her family and said. "I can sure see why a paleontologist would want to be stationed out here."

The Parkers drove back to the visitor center. "A perfect time to get out of the sun," Dad mentioned. There they watched the park movie and toured the displays, learning more about the Badlands, its animals, the fossils found in the region, and the early explorers of the area.

Afterwards Morgan, James, Mom, and Dad went into camp and lay low for the remainder of the afternoon, waiting in their tent for the heat to subside and the sun's intensity to wane.

While in the tent, James pulled out his journal.

This is James Parker reporting.

There must have been a whole lot going on here about thirty-three or so million years ago. We just toured the visitor center and all their fossil displays. The prehistoric mammals of the region were incredible!

And I think we may have discovered the fossil remains of a bunch of them. We may also have reported the theft of the remains of some more.

I hope they catch those two guys, those bone-fossil thieves. It was pretty eerie witnessing them get away with a trunkful of rocks, which were really fossils, at least we think.

Speaking of getting away, we will be on our way, tomorrow over to the Black Hills and its many attractions, but most of all to Wind Cave and Mount Rushmore.

More soon from South Dakota!

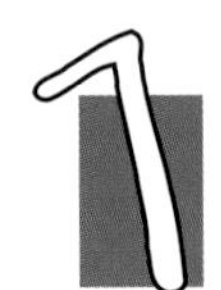

The Prairie Dog Whisperer

Later that afternoon the Parkers left camp and headed out on the Badlands scenic drive. As they drove west, the prairie grasses on the right waved with the wind and the buttes and peaks of the Badlands pointed toward the sky on their left.

The road weaved in and around the heart of the Badlands and over a couple of passes. They pulled over at Yellow Mounds overlook so Morgan could take some pictures of the yellowish bands of clay among the badlands. Then Mom turned down the dirt road toward Conata Picnic area.

Color bands in the clay

Once there the Parkers piled out and inspected the area around where the "Pig Dig" had occurred.

The National Park Service and cooperating scientists recently completed a multi-year dig at Badlands called the Pig Dig. The name was derived from fossils discovered there that were initially believed to be from an ancient piglike animal called an *Archaeotherium.* Later those bones were proven to be from a hornless rhino-like creature called a *Subhyracodon,* but the name stuck anyway. In the end both ancient rhinos and pigs were found at the site.

The dig started in 1993 when two visitors from Iowa saw a large backbone sticking out of the ground near the Conata Picnic area. The dig eventually led to the excavation of more than nineteen thousand bones and it took fifteen years. Remains from up to eighteen species were discovered at the dig, including a bobcat-sized saber-toothed cat, turtles, tiny deerlike animals, *Mesohippus, Archaeotherium,* and the *Subhyracodon.*

Some of the specimens were partially articulated, meaning the animal skeletons were partially intact, which is very rare. Other fossils were found isolated from the rest of the animal's remains. With so much all in one place, paleontologists believe the site was probably a prehistoric watering hole and many of the animals got trapped in the mud, leading to their deaths.

Due to the abundant remains there, scientists now have a better understanding of how fossils are preserved and how bones accumulate in one area.

Visitors at the Pig Dig

"It's unbelievable how much they found out here," Mom said. "The hills seem so barren now."

"I wonder what will end up happening with what we discovered," Morgan said.

"I guess we'll know a little more about that tomorrow," Dad added.

After wandering around the Conata area, Morgan, James, Mom, and Dad returned to their car. Their next stop was the crowded Pinnacles overlook.

There's color in them hills!

Once there Mom noticed all the parked cars and people wandering around. "There must be quite a view from here," Mom mentioned while pulling in and looking for a spot to park.

A moment later the family left the car and meandered along various short pathways to views overlooking the badlands. At one spot the family gazed down at a dense juniper forest. A sign there pointed out some of the birds of the area.

"Townsend solitaire, rosy finch, tree sparrow, northern shrike, and bluebird," James read some of the names.

But Morgan noticed a large gathering of people near the end of the path. "I think something's out there," she exclaimed.

The Parkers hurried over. The views at this overlook were into the wild, expansive badlands. But some people were gazing far below, while others used binoculars.

James was the first of the family to spot a couple of large, tan-colored animals. "Look!" he pointed.

A few bighorn sheep were scattered among the buttes and bluffs well below the Pinnacles area. One appeared to be nibbling on grass. Another seemed to be staring back up the slope toward the onlookers. A third bighorn was picking its way along a rocky bluff.

After observing the bighorns at the Pinnacles overlook, the Parkers returned to their car. They drove on, reaching a gravel road a short time later.

James checked the map. "Yep. That's still the scenic drive," he noted.

Mom watched a few cars drive along the dirt. Then she checked the sky. "The weather is certainly cooperating for us today."

Mom turned onto the gravel road. She drove slower as the family continued to gaze out the windows and admire the scenery.

Here the prairie was broken into drier, dustier patches with less vegetation. James was the first to notice small mounds of dirt scattered about.

Prairie dog mound

Prairie dog hole

Mom saw a small furry animal on top of one of the mounds. She slowed down. "Look!" she pointed excitedly. "Prairie dogs!"

Some stood on the dirt piles. Every once in a while one would bound across the prairie to another mound. A few were close to the road but when the Parkers drove by they dashed into their holes and disappeared.

Soon the family reached a small parking area. The Parkers pulled over and piled out to examine the Roberts Prairie Dog Town.

The area around here was flat and grassy with small piles of dirt scattered throughout. Prairie dogs were all around barking, calling to each other, and keeping an eye on the Parkers and a few other visitors watching them.

Mom took several steps away from the car and into the "town." Morgan stayed a few feet behind Mom. One prairie dog was fairly close, perched right on top of a little pile of dried dirt.

Both Morgan and Mom slowly inched nearer, trying to get a close-up view and better pictures. Finally, once they were about twenty feet away from the hole, Mom kneeled down to appear less threatening.

The prairie dog watched Mom while twitching and glancing about nervously. Mom slowly lifted her arm to gesture to Morgan to stay still but the prairie dog, startled by the movement, dashed halfway into its hole. Morgan took the opportunity to come up to Mom while James and Dad stayed distant.

Gradually the prairie dog became more comfortable with the two onlookers. It stood back on top of its mound on its hind feet and twitched its nose in the direction of Morgan and Mom. Then it barked several high-pitched whistle-like sounds.

How about a little kiss?

Mom tried communicating with the brown, furry animal. "It's okay," she said calmly. Then mom made a few soft clicking sounds.

Mom turned back toward Dad. "Just call me the prairie dog whisperer," she said with a smile.

Dad replied. "I don't mean to break up the session, but did you see what else is out there?"

Morgan jumped up. "Where?"

The prairie dog immediately dashed all the way into its hole.

Then Mom also got up. "Well, enough of that."

AN UNDERGROUND WORLD

Prairie dogs are members of the squirrel family. Their colonies once numbered in the hundreds of millions, possibly up to a billion, making them one of the most abundant mammals in North America. Now only about 5 percent of their original numbers remain, for a variety of reasons. Prairie dogs live in complex colonies with networks of tunnels and a wide variety of openings. Raised burrow entrances indicate a colony is around and these raised areas also give the prairie dogs, which are typically only twelve inches tall, extra height when acting as guards or sentries. Tunnels in the colony have separate rooms for sleeping, raising babies, storing food, and eliminating waste. Prairie dog communication is highly complex and includes high-pitched warning barks that signal that different types of predators are near.

James and Dad pointed toward a small herd of buffalo in the distance. The five large animals were scattered about, nibbling on grass or lying down.

Dad sighed. "I love the Badlands!"

Just then a ranger truck pulled up. The two rangers inside spent some time sifting through gear in the back of the cab, then, finally, exited the vehicle.

Meanwhile as the sun slowly sank behind the intricately eroded badlands to the west, the Parkers wandered back to their car, which was parked right next to the rangers. Morgan, James, Mom, and Dad got in, but Mom noticed large spotlights among the rangers' supplies. Because of the incident with the bone thieves earlier, that got the Parkers' attention. Mom rolled down her window, leaned out, and asked, "We're just a bit curious. What are you looking for out here?"

"Black-footed ferrets," one of the rangers answered. "They're a protected species at the park and were once nearly extinct. They're extremely reclusive and highly nocturnal. We do know they eat prairie dogs, though, and that's probably why the animals you see around here are so skittish. This is prime black-footed ferret habitat. In order to see how they are doing, we have to hang out here at night."

James then asked, "Do you see them with those flashlights?"

"Spotlights," the ranger replied. "And, yes, we shine them out here at night into the prairie dog town. Ferrets also hang out in burrows, but every once in a while they'll pop their heads up. These spotlights catch their eyes in the light. From a distance their eyes look distinctly emerald green. And there is no doubt we've spotted a ferret when we see that.

Sometimes, their curiosity allows us to get closer. They want to see what's behind the light. Many of the ferret have been pit-tagged, meaning we've got a computer chip in them that we can read with this device." The ranger held up a donut-shaped receiver. "We stick it right over a hole and if we get a signal, we know a ferret is down there."

"Even with all that," the other ranger added, "we have to be pretty lucky to spot one. Although we now know there are about twenty black-footed ferrets living out here at Robert's Prairie Dog Town."

"What a great job!" Mom said. "I wish we could go out tonight with you."

"Yes, definitely," Morgan added.

The Parkers said good-bye to the rangers and drove west for one more stop at the Sage Creek Basin overlook. There the badlands were vast and expansive, stretching far out into the distant, wilderness horizon.

The family stood there, and then meandered down a few feet on a social trail toward a clump of sunflowers nestled near a tree. "Can you imagine if all of our lands looked as wild and as natural as this?" Mom said.

"Well, at least America has these national parks," Dad added. "So we can still get glimpses of the wild."

After a few moments at Sage Creek, the Parkers remorsefully returned to their car. They drove east, retracing their path, and barely had enough time to make it to the Cedar Pass Lodge cafe for dinner before it closed. This time there were no storm chasers.

Sunflowers at the Badlands

Returning to the Past

With no note left at camp to tell them otherwise, the Parkers got up early, right after sunrise. They packed everything up while the air was fresh and cool, and the sky dotted with a few solitary wispy clouds. In the distance the badlands silhouetted the soft blue morning sky.

"The best time of day," Dad commented as he tore down the tent.

"You said that about the evening a few days ago," James reminded Dad.

"Oh yeah. It's a tie then."

At a quarter to seven the Parkers were all set to go, their rental car stuffed with gear. They drove the short distance to the familiar parking lot at the Fossil Exhibit Trail. When they arrived, Eric was waiting outside a car and another person was with him.

"Good morning!" Eric greeted the Parkers as they all walked up. He then introduced Rachel Benton, the park's chief paleontologist.

"Hi," Morgan and James replied in unison.

"Are you all ready to lead us to some fossils?" Rachel added.

"You bet," Mom replied.

The six hikers walked in a single-file line back to the discovery on the Castle Trail. Birds flitted about and the comfortably warm morning sun basked on the badlands formations.

After a while James asked. "Did you find out any more about that suspicious car?"

"We did what we could," Eric replied. "The only people allowed to search for fossils out here are those with permits. And that party did not have one. We turned in all your information to the authorities. So from here on it's a law enforcement matter. We really appreciate you letting us know what you saw. Fossils are so very important to both science and education."

Then Rachel added, "It's illegal to collect fossils without a research permit signed by the park superintendent. Its part of the Paleontological Preservation Act, signed into law in March 2009. Among other things, that law states that the collecting of vertebrate fossils can be done on federal lands by permit only, so this was a criminal act."

Finally, Rachel said, "Taking fossils in some ways is like taking pieces away from a jigsaw puzzle. Without the missing pieces we'll never see the whole picture and have a chance to know everything about that animal and its ancient ecosystem."

Morgan and James began to slow down. "We're getting close!" Morgan announced with excitement.

A few steps later, James burst out, "It's right down there."

James led Rachel and Eric off the trail. Morgan, Mom, and Dad followed. Quickly they all gathered at the edge of the gully. James clambered into the miniature canyon and bent down. About halfway up, along the side, and also on top of the stream-cut edge, the bed of fossils still stuck out of the rock. James smiled, then looked up at the two rangers. "They're still here. I was a little worried, especially because of the poaching we saw yesterday."

Rachel climbed down. She edged closer to the find and inspected it. As she did a smile spread across her face. Then Rachel slipped off her pack, unzipped it and pulled out a hand lens. She studied the fossils closely with the magnifying glass. "These aren't just for science classes," Rachel mentioned, holding the lens up.

Rachel looked over the permineralized bones and murmured, "This is really something!"

"What is it?" Morgan asked, moving closer.

"Well, from what I can tell, this one here is a large part of a jaw of a plant eater," Rachel looked some more. "Wait. Hold on a second."

Rachel again reached into her pack. This time she pulled out a small paintbrush. She used it to dust off any loose dirt she could find on the multimillion-year-old object.

"Look here," Rachel said enthusiastically, "these stained, blackish-brown teeth, or at least what I can see of them, are flat, made for eating plants."

"And over here. Yep. This is a tortoise shell. The shell is partially squashed due to all the weight on it for millions of years. But tortoises are the most common of all the fossils found in the Badlands."

"We saw some of those displayed at the visitor center," Dad recalled.

Now Eric stepped into the tiny gully. He walked around the immediate area and began inspecting the fossils. "It's quite a conglomeration here!" he announced.

While Eric and the Parkers searched in and around the gully, Rachel took out a notebook and a GPS device. She began jotting down information in her book and using the GPS to help her pinpoint the exact location of the discovery. After a few minutes of searching, James walked over and asked, "What are you writing?"

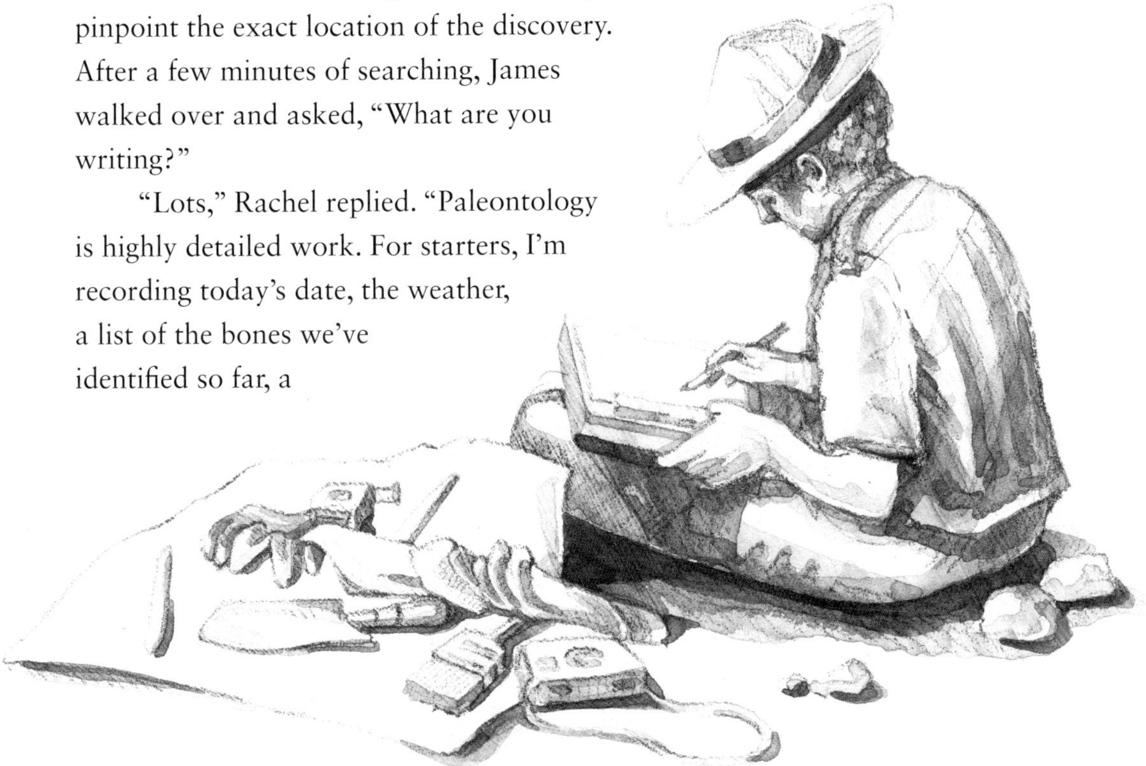

"Lots," Rachel replied. "Paleontology is highly detailed work. For starters, I'm recording today's date, the weather, a list of the bones we've identified so far, a description of the bones, and the angle they are embedded in the rock. Then I noted the location. I drew a little map of the area." Rachel reached into her pack and pulled out a camera. "Now we've got to take a bunch of pictures."

Rachel began snapping photos, which grabbed Morgan's attention. She came over, held her camera up, and said, "You are welcome to use ours."

"Thank you," Rachel replied. "Your pictures, I hear, led Eric to get all of us back out here today. And it's a good thing they did. But, now I have to take a ton of photos and organize them into a grid of the area for the beginning of our documentation. And it's quite a lot we'll end up doing. Just what we can see on the surface represents an amazing find!"

James inched closer. "So you're not going to dig them out of the ground?"

"We will, yes, but that's not likely today. We may get to one or two. But, for a proper dig we'll need to initiate a whole excavation process. We'll need partners and grants to do that, and a wide variety of equipment and experts to help out. We'll eventually get that going, and once we do, we could be out here a long time."

"Like the Pig Dig!" Morgan recalled.

"Exactly. Depending on what we find."

After some time photographing and documenting, Rachel called out excitedly, "Well, look at this!"

Everyone stopped what they were doing and crowded around the paleontologist. She pointed toward an area on a jaw she had just dusted off. "See this crushed indentation at the front of the jaw? That's a scar. Something happened to this animal, which is a *Mesohippus,* possibly just before it died. It looks like it got a tooth bite right into its jaw."

"You mean another animal killed it?" James wondered.

"It could be," Rachel answered. "Of course, we'll never know for sure. But we do know it suffered a serious enough injury to permanently damage facial bones."

Finally, both Rachel and Eric took one more long inspection of the vicinity. Then they climbed out of the gully and brushed themselves off.

Rachel looked at the Parkers. "What we have started today is just the beginning. Thank you so much for taking us out here." Then Rachel looked at Morgan, James, Mom, and Dad.

"So what are your plans for the day?" Rachel asked.

Mom answered. "We're on our way to Wind Cave. We've reserved a Candlelight Tour this afternoon."

"Oh, you'll love it," Rachel said. "But you'd better get going. It's several hours away."

"Can we find out later what was discovered out here?" Morgan asked.

"Of course," Rachel replied. "After all, you're the ones who initiated it."

The Parkers gave Rachel and Eric their e-mail addresses. They shook hands and said good-bye.

Then, begrudgingly, Morgan, James, Mom, and Dad began their trek back to the car. For the first part of the hike, Morgan and James kept glancing back to see what Rachel and Eric were doing. But all they could see were the tops of their heads bobbing about the gully. And soon they were out of sight altogether.

A while later the Parkers were back at their car. The family piled in and drove west toward the Black Hills. As they headed out of the park, along the scenic drive, Morgan, James, Mom, and Dad gazed out the window at the eroded badlands.

"It's so hard to leave here," Mom admitted.

"So true," Dad said. "So true."

The scenic drive

A Little Cave History

After leaving the Badlands, the Parkers drove west on Highway 90 toward Rapid City. Just before town they took Highway 79 south. The Black Hills loomed in the western horizon.

As they drove toward Wind Cave National Park, Mom shared some stories. "I remember hearing of someone who once got lost in Wind Cave," she mentioned. "It took a search party thirty-six hours to find her."

"How did she get lost?" James asked.

"She went exploring behind a rock without marking her way back."

"You mean with string or something?" Morgan replied.

"Exactly," Mom answered. "Something that indicates a clear path back to the group but is easy to clean up and doesn't damage the cave."

"How did they finally find her then?" Dad chimed in.

"She exhausted her voice while yelling for help and picked up a rock and kept tapping it against the cave walls. Someone in the search party heard that and they were eventually able to locate her."

"Wow," Dad responded. "I hope she was okay. Thirty-six hours is a long time to be lost in a cave, or anywhere for that matter. I guess that's a lesson for all of us to stay with our group."

Then Mom shared more. "I did some of my own exploring about Wind Cave on the Internet when we were at home. Caving fascinates me and I used to go spelunking in California as part of a grotto club in college. So I spent some time looking up the history of Wind Cave." Mom paused to gauge her family's interest.

"And?" Dad asked curiously.

"First of all, it became a national park in 1903. It's the seventh national park in our system and the first one to protect a cave. But the discovery of Wind Cave actually began in earnest when a kid, really, named Alvin McDonald began exploring passages when he was only sixteen. His whole story is quite interesting."

Morgan and James leaned forward from the back seat.

Mom took a deep breath and gathered her thoughts. "I found some of his diary entries online. That's right, you two," Mom spoke to the twins. "He kept a diary of his adventures! And he wrote about his caving expeditions. One thing that I learned was his secret code that he inscribed on parts of the cave. ZUQ . . ."

"I wonder what that stands for," James mused.

"He wrote his signature or code on more than fifty passages inside the cave," Mom went on. "By the time he was twenty he had explored about ten miles of cave passages, and he even gave tours underground."

"Ten miles!" James exclaimed. "That's a huge cave."

"Yes it is," Mom replied. "But they've now found over one hundred thirty-six miles of cave there. It's currently the fourth longest cave in the world."

"And I hear they're still exploring more," Dad said.

"Back to Alvin," Mom continued. "Unfortunately he died at the age of twenty due to typhoid fever, but he and his caving partners sure were interesting."

"What did they do?" James asked.

Mom paused from talking to watch the highway. They approached the 101 junction and Mom turned west toward the Black Hills and Wind Cave. Then she continued.

"Alvin's family, the McDonalds, and another family, the Stablers, owned the rights to Wind Cave and they wanted to promote tourism there. They tried some schemes including one with a famous mind reader named Paul Alexander Johnstone.

"Apparently this Johnstone guy was so good at mind reading that to promote the cave and get more people to visit, the McDonalds and the Stablers set up a publicity stunt with him. They hid a small hat pin somewhere within the cave." Mom paused to emphasize, "Mind you there's more than ten miles of known cave passages at this point. So this guy Johnstone, then, was going to go down in the cave and find the hat pin just by reading the mind of the person who hid it."

"Hey, I kind of read ranger Eric's mind in the Badlands," James recalled.

Mom smiled. "Yes, you did."

"So," James leaned forward in his seat. "What happened then? Did he find it?"

Mom saw a junction up ahead and slowed the car down. "There's our next turn-off," she announced.

Mom headed north on Highway 385, just south of the park boundary. Mom purposely didn't answer James's question, but still continued talking about Wind Cave. "I also went onto the park's website to find some of the names of the cave rooms."

"The people who explored and discovered each room get to name them, right?" Dad asked.

"Exactly. So I don't know if these are newly named rooms, or some of the old, original ones. But here are a few names I remember: A.F. McDonald room, the Air Tube, Alligator, Angel's Wings, Antarctica, Applehead, and Arm Pit."

Morgan and James laughed at that one.

"And those are only a few of the ones listed that start with A," Mom added.

"Maybe we should skip the Arm Pit room," James concluded.

"Oh yeah, and Attic," Mom remembered one more.

"I can only imagine what each of those rooms looks like," Dad said

Finally the Parkers drove past the Wind Cave park boundary sign. Just ahead was a small traffic jam of cars. And in the nearby fields was a herd of bison. Mom pulled the car over and the family got out and watched the two-thousand-pound animals graze on the prairie grasses.

"I guess it's not just caves that this park is all about," Dad mentioned.

Meanwhile James looked over the park map. "The caves are just ahead at the visitor center," he realized.

Dad also glanced at the map. "That means," Dad thought aloud, "that we're probably standing directly above some of the one hundred thirty-six miles of cave passages right now."

"I wonder if there are people down there," Morgan exclaimed.

The Parkers watched the bison for a few more minutes. Then they drove on, taking the side road to the visitor center. The large parking lot was loaded with cars. The family parked, then walked past the flagpole and into the building.

Once inside, Morgan, James, Mom, and Dad stopped and took in all the hubbub. An information desk crowded with people was just to the left and the gift shop was to the right. Straight ahead, stairs led down to cave tours and a museum of displays. At the back of the room, people were in a line buying cave tour tickets.

Meanwhile, a ranger announced, "The Natural Entrance Tour meets outside the building, down the stairs at the shelter in five minutes!"

Mom went to the front desk first to check in. She then proceeded to the back to get their tickets. "We'll meet you downstairs," Dad said as he, James, and Morgan went to learn about the park and look at the displays.

A few minutes later, Mom came down holding up four tickets. "Our tour is in a little less than an hour at one thirty," she said.

After a few more minutes at the museum, the Parkers left to go set up their tent at the campground just up the road. They ate a quick lunch at the picnic table there, then drove back just before the tour got started.

Lights Out Underground

"The Candlelight Tour is meeting now right by the water fountain," a ranger called out.

Morgan jumped up from her seat in the lobby. "That's us!"

The Parkers walked toward the ranger. He waited for the full group to gather and counted. "Great, ten; everyone's here." Then he led them all outside.

Soon the group was in front of a door. The ranger opened it and brought out a few small boxes with piles of gloves inside. "Okay, everybody, choose a pair that fits."

Each person looked for a pair of gloves. Then the ranger passed out silver buckets, each with a candle in it.

The ranger looked toward the group. "Welcome to the Candlelight Tour. This is my favorite way to see the cave, the old-fashioned way, just like Alvin McDonald and the early explorers did."

The ranger studied his companions of the next two hours.

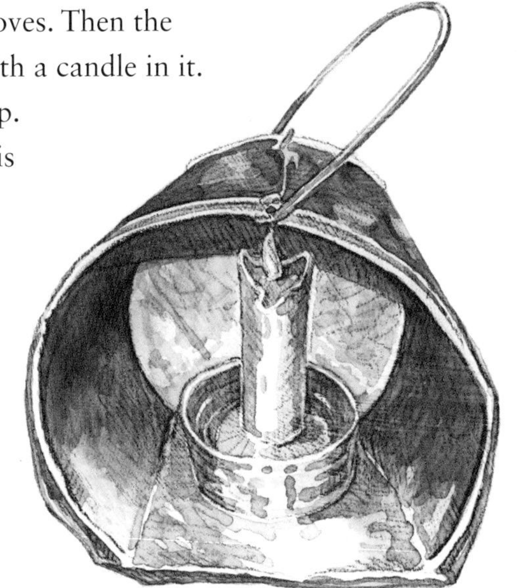

"We're going to spend some quality, intimate time together, so we ought to get to know each other. I'll start. I'm Wendell, and I'm from here in South Dakota. I like to call South Dakota 'fly-over country' because most people fly right over us as they go from coast to coast. Well, anyway, when it's not summer, I'm a high-school biology teacher. So how about all of you?"

A person from each group introduced themselves and their companions. There were people from New York, Florida, Michigan, and Indiana. When it came to the Parkers, James did the honors. "I'm James and this is my twin sister, Morgan. This is my dad, Robert, and my mom, Kristen. We're from California and it's my sister's and my first time in a cave. My mom, though, has been spelunking before."

Wendell smiled. "A spelunker from the west coast. Well, welcome everyone." Then he said. "Our journey starts the easiest way possible. Follow me."

Wendell led the group toward an elevator. He pressed a button and waited. A moment later the doors opened. "Come on in," Wendell gestured.

The natural cave entrance

The group did and the doors shut. Wendell pressed the inside button and the elevator began its descent.

Soon the cave transportation system stopped and the doors opened again. Wendell guided the group through a small underground room and onto a lighted pathway within the cave.

Finally Wendell looked everyone over and announced, "Welcome to Wind Cave!" Then he said sheepishly, "I know it's not the natural entrance. But you wouldn't want to go in that way anyway. It's a very small hole the size of a round cowboy hat. You can see it along the pathway on the Natural Entrance Tour. But even those cave visitors don't go in through that hole."

Wendell explained further. "Yes, we've made it a little easier for visitors to get in and out of the cave, but beyond here, outside of our pathway, everything has been kept natural. But when Jesse Bingham found the natural entrance around 1881 and peeked in, it blew his hat away. The next time he tried it, the hat got sucked in. You can imagine his reaction! It's air pressure changes outside the cave that cause the wind in the cave to blow one way or another. We have even measured it up to seventy-five miles per hour. So now you know where this cave got its name. Does anyone know what else Wind Cave is famous for?"

"Boxwork," someone in the group called out.

"Precisely," Wendell replied. "Boxwork is a unique formation found almost exclusively here at Wind Cave. I'll tell you more about it soon. But keep your eyes out for it along the trail, and follow me."

Wendell led the group down a cemented and well-lit path. The ten visitors snaked along underground until Wendell called from up front. "Okay, everyone, move to the side."

A much larger group of cave tourers was coming in the opposite direction. The Parkers and others stepped to the right and let the long line of people go by.

Morgan whispered to James. "None of them have candle buckets."

"Or gloves," James added.

Soon Wendell led everyone past a steel gate. "Head down our special stairs," he announced.

One by one each person did. Then Wendell locked the gate behind him and clambered down to meet the group. "Okay," he beamed. "It's time for the fun to begin."

"Please hold your buckets straight out," Wendell instructed. "That way wax doesn't drip on the cave anywhere."

Wendell walked up to each person and lit his or her candle.

As the Parkers waited, Dad leaned over to James and his family. "This whole mind-reading thing you've been talking about has piqued my curiosity," he shared. "So I'm wondering if any of you can read my mind now."

Morgan, James, and Mom thought for a moment. Then Morgan blurted out. "You want to go spelunking, too?" she guessed.

Dad laughed. "You almost got it. I was thinking just that a minute ago. Right when you said that, though, I was listening to my stomach grumble. I'm really hungry!"

Mom laughed. "I could have guessed that!"

Then James smiled. "Can you read my mind?"

Wendell walked up and attempted to answer James. "Well, I just met you, of course, but my guess is you want to be a cave explorer using these cave buckets just like Alvin McDonald."

James beamed. "Hey—you read my mind!" Then he added, "I was also wondering what secret code I would have used to mark my signature."

"That's what I was thinking," Morgan interjected. "And I came up with one: MJP."

"What does that stand for?" Wendell asked.

"Morgan and James Parker."

"I assume that's the two of you," Wendell replied, and then he finished lighting everyone's candle.

Next, Wendell walked over to a switch. "Okay, are all of you ready?" Wendell flicked the switch and the lights went out. He announced, "Welcome to Wind Cave the way Alvin McDonald and others saw it. Go ahead and shine your buckets around and check out the cave by candlelight."

After a few minutes Wendell said, "So, back in the days when there were no computers, iPods, cell phones, or cable TV, sixteen-year-olds like Alvin at least had this cave to explore."

Wendell added, "Now, I have some bad news and some good news for all of you. What would you like first?"

"The bad news!" James called out.

"All right," Wendell replied. "The bad news is cave exploring will not make anyone rich. There is no money to go spelunking down here, or in any other cave."

"And the good news?" another person asked.

"The good news is anyone can do this. If you join a grotto and learn the proper techniques and have the right equipment, we can all become cave explorers and go, potentially, where no man—or woman—has gone before. Okay," Wendell pointed his light forward. "Keep your buckets flat to help you see straight ahead and follow me."

And the group did, quickly leaving the cemented path behind and stepping onto the dirt and rocks on the natural and uneven cave floor.

The Parkers, Wendell, and the others on the Candlelight Tour trekked along. At one point Mom lifted her bucket, illuminating the cave walls with a shadowy, dim light. "Seeing a cave by candlelight is so much different than a lighted, cemented pathway," she mentioned.

The tour led the cavers past an area with some boxwork. Each person studied the unique formation composed of thin blades of hardened minerals hanging from the cave ceiling in mazes of box-like patterns. Wendell pointed out, "Look for some brown, black, and blue colors in the boxwork. That's the mineral manganese in the rock. It gives these boxes a bluish tint, and because of that we call this area the Blue Grotto."

Morgan's candlelight captured a glimpse of crystals flashing along a rock wall. "Look!" she whispered to James. And the twins studied the tiny, shiny minerals embedded in the rock.

Wind Cave's famous Box Work

The tour continued. At times, Mom and Dad and other adults had to duck and maneuver to get past, under, or around natural rock barriers. But in those places, Morgan and James just walked on through.

Dad grunted and held the base of his back after straightening up in one such place. Then he looked at his kids. "Spelunking might just be an endeavor for the young," he mentioned, half jokingly.

The group passed a number 82 etched on one of the cave walls. Wendell called out from up front. "That's a survey marker from 1902, the year before this was made into a national park. You might have also seen some pieces of string around. Those were placed here by explorers or the Civilian Conservation Corp to help mark their way back out of the cave."

Walking on the uneven surface, underground, and by candlelight was slow going. At times, each person had to shine their light backward to help others see potential hazardous obstacles in their paths.

Soon Wendell stopped again and pointed above. "It's a tight squeeze ahead," he announced. "And it's especially narrow at the bottom. A real potential ankle grabber. I'm going to go first and then call out 'clear' once I make it through. Then, one at a time I'd like all of you to do the same."

One by one those on the tour proceeded. Finally it was the Parkers' turn. Mom went first, followed by James, Morgan, and Dad.

Once they were all past the tight spot, the group gathered in a larger room. "Welcome to the Tabernacle," Wendell announced. "We're going to do a full circle in this room and return. So look around and see if you'll be able to figure out when we are back here."

Each person tried to pick out some features in the underground maze they would be able to recognize later, when they returned.

Then Wendell gestured. "Let's everyone find a stable place to sit or stand. I want to show you what a cave really looks like."

The guide looked at each person and smiled. "Are you all ready?"

Everyone nodded.

Wendell blew out his candle. "Okay, all of you do the same."

Each person blew out his or her light. Soon it was completely pitch black. Wendell stayed silent a moment, then whispered, "Now you are seeing what every other cave in the world looks like.

"There really is no place on earth where you can experience absolute darkness except in a cave, or at the very bottom of a deep ocean, and I doubt any of us will be visiting there any time soon. Caves are a bit easier to get to."

Wendell took a deep breath. "Would you like to hear a little story?"

A few people said, "Yes. Great."

Wendell told the story about the mind reader that Mom had shared earlier. He ended it by informing the group that, "The mind reader found the hat pin. And when he came out of the cave there was a big news story about the event. It was quite a frenzy."

"So he read Alvin McDonald's mind!" Morgan exclaimed.

"Or whoever hid the pin," Dad added.

James leaned over toward Mom and said, "How did you know they were going to talk about that?"

"I didn't," Mom replied, smiling, but no one saw it.

Finally, Wendell said. "Okay, raise your hand if you want me to turn the lights back on."

Everyone laughed again.

"Well before I bring us back into the light," Wendell said into the darkness, "How do you think we'd get out of here if we didn't have any light source?"

"Scream!" some replied.

"Crawl until I found the passage out," another said.

"Pray," someone else answered.

"Well, thankfully, none of those options is going to be necessary," Wendell said. He flicked on his lighter, lit his candle, and then proceeded to light the others.

Soon everyone was trekking along again. The ranger led the group right next to a formation hanging down from the cave's ceiling. "This," he pointed with his candlelight, "is what we call the Eagle's Talon. It's where the hat pin was hidden and then found by the mind reader."

Everyone looked at the tiny hole as they walked by.

James mentioned to Morgan as he passed, "I wonder if I hid something in here if you'd be able to find it. You *always* say you know what I'm thinking."

"I think that's because we're twins," Morgan replied. "But even so, with a hundred thirty-six miles of cave, don't count on me to be a very good mind reader down here!"

Wendell again gathered the group. Then he pointed with his light. "We've got some nice formations of boxwork in here that you might want to take a look at while you're hanging out. Meanwhile I'm going to have all of you wait here while I take three of you at a time to a very special, extremely delicate cave formation."

BOXING UP THE CAVE

No other cave in the world has as much or as well-formed boxwork as Wind Cave. Boxwork consists of blades of calcite hanging or projecting from cave walls or ceilings. The calcite blades or fins crisscross in boxlike patterns, giving the formation its name. What forms boxwork is not completely understood. But part of the process is that erosion-resistant calcite fins stayed in place over the eons, while highly erodable limestone rock that once filled in the gaps within the boxes dissolved over time, leaving the maze of boxes seen in the cave now.

The Parkers looked at the cave's intricately woven erratic patterns of boxes. They shone their candles here and there, studying the unique features. But soon, Morgan and Dad went with one group and James and Mom another to a special room. While there, Wendell pointed to some tiny white crystals conglomerating like miniature frosty hairs or gathered snowflakes on the cave's ceiling.

"Frost!" James said when he saw the tiny features.

"It sure looks like it," Wendell agreed. "But it's not cold enough for frost down here. What it is, though, is a very rare, extremely delicate cave formation called frostwork."

Frostwork at Wind Cave

"Is that why we can only go down here three at a time?" Morgan asked when she was there with Dad.

"Pretty much so," Wendell replied. "In some cases, although not here, the crystal strands from this kind of formation can grow several feet long, or even longer, hanging in the air like hair for thousands of years. Even breathing in a cave room with those in them can destroy the formation. But here it's a small room and we want all of you to be able to get a good look at the formation without feeling crowded, or possibly bumping into anything so fragile. You can see why we treat it with extreme care."

Mom gawked. "It sure is beautiful."

Once everyone had seen the frostwork, Wendell led the group farther through the underground maze. A moment later, Morgan called out excitedly, "We're back in the Tabernacle!"

"Precisely," Wendell replied. "How did you know?"

"I recognized that big flat rock over there."

"Sounds like we have ourselves a spelunker in the group."

Morgan smiled.

Soon Wendell brought everyone back to some stairs. The group scaled them, then Wendell locked the gate behind before giving out a bit more information. "We know a great deal about Alvin McDonald's caving because he kept a diary of his journeys."

Dad whispered to the twins. "See how important it is to keep a journal?"

"All right everyone," Wendell called out once the group was back on the cemented, lighted path. "You can blow out your candles."

Each person did, and then they clambered on through the more developed part of the cave, enjoying the smooth path and its lit features.

Soon they returned to the elevator and piled in. A few seconds later they exited to a bright, sunlit world. Once outside, everyone returned their gloves to the boxes.

The Parkers thanked Wendell and took the path to the visitor center. They spent some time there, and at the gift shop, eventually returning to their car and their campsite for the evening.

After another day at the park, the next evening, Morgan wrote in her journal.

Dear Diary:

My family is now afflicted with "cave-itis." After our candlelight tour of Wind Cave yesterday, we've now also done the Natural Entrance and the Fairgrounds Tours. On our way out of here tomorrow, we're going to stop at nearby Jewel Cave, too. It seems like, lately, we're spending more time going underground than above. At least then we don't have to wear sunscreen!

Too bad we can't go spelunking though. You have to be at least sixteen, here, to go. Funny, that was Alvin McDonald's age when he started cave exploring here. James says it's not fair because since we're younger, and smaller, we're perfectly suited to wild caving experiences.

I also think we might be more flexible and would explore some of the cave's tight passages (of which there are plenty!) easier. But either way, we'll just have to come back.

Anyway, we're spending a few days enjoying the *many* sights in and around the Black Hills, while staying camped at Wind Cave, where there's more to see than caves, including bison, prairie dogs, and a nice hike we've been on, too. The day after tomorrow we head out to our vacation's grand finale destination—Mount Rushmore. Teddy Roosevelt, we'll see you soon!

Sincerely,
Morgan Parker

On the Presidential Trail

Traffic patrol waved the Parkers toward the parking garage. Dad pulled into the underground structure packed with cars. As he looked for a spot, Morgan, James, and Mom noticed license plates from all over the country.

"There's one from New York!" Morgan announced.

"And Florida," James added, picking out a state even farther away.

Then Dad said, "Here's one from our home state, California."

Finally, Dad found a spot to park. The family slid out and then headed up toward the patriotic mountain.

The Parkers, along with tons of other people, climbed a set of stairs toward the monument. Many of Mount Rushmore's visitors wore patriotic attire for the Fourth of July holiday. There were Uncle Sam hats; small flags on strollers; red, white, and blue T-shirts; and other holiday gear adorning the visitors.

Mom looked around. "We picked quite a day to be at Mount Rushmore," she commented.

The family stopped to check out the visitor center, then headed toward the Presidential Trail.

The wide path along the way was adorned with the flags of the fifty-six states, districts, commonwealths, and territories. As they proceeded, the Parkers found the brown bear and star on the California state flag. Morgan got her family to stand beneath their flag while she snapped a photo.

Eventually the Parkers came to a large amphitheatre facing the massive, monumental mountain. Morgan, James, Mom, and Dad, along with hordes of others, stood there gazing at the stone replicas of the former presidents. "Wow!" Dad exclaimed in awe. "Those carvings are huge!"

"And so realistic," Mom added.

Morgan took a bunch of pictures of the mountain from different angles.

Then the family gazed down at the large outdoor amphitheatre. "This is where we're going to watch the lighting of the presidents' faces tonight!" Mom announced.

"I can't wait," Morgan added.

The family stood and people-watched, both the hustle and bustle of the tourists from all over the country, and the absolute still of the stone presidential monument above.

Morgan noticed two men, far below on the seats of the amphitheatre. One, a man with a red hat on, stood up on a long wooden plank and balanced on one foot while laughing. He put each arm out and announced something that Morgan couldn't quite hear. But she did catch the last word, "rich." Then the man walked over to his friend and gave him a high five.

His friend laughed and they both dashed up the steps and headed toward the Presidential Trail.

Morgan sensed familiarity in the two men. She looked at her family to see if they, too, had recognized them and noticed their antics. But Mom and Dad were either gazing at the presidents, or watching other people nearby. And James seemed to be fixated on someone carrying a soft vanilla ice cream cone. He delivered a message to Mom and Dad by looking but not saying a word.

Dad eventually got the drift. "Soon," he said to James with a grin, "after our walk."

From there the Parkers headed out on the main walkway onto the Presidential Trail.

As the family strolled along the famed path, they got closer and closer to the former presidents. Some of the visitors were listening to headsets, an audio tour of the trail at designated stops.

At one point, Mom gazed in the opposite direction, back toward the east and the Black Hills as they sank toward the plains. "Now I can see where these mountains got their name," she said. "All the trees when viewed at a distance make this mountain island look dark or black."

Soon the Parkers came to a small side area with Lakota Indian displays depicting their way of life. The Parkers walked into the mock miniature village. "It was actually their home here," Dad said, "before we decided to carve up the mountain and make it one of our national parks."

Morgan, James, Mom, and Dad wandered around, looking over the displays in the village. Lakota and Cherokee interpreters were on hand to

The Lakota way of life

explain various techniques regarding their culture and heritage. There was a demonstration on how to build a tipi. A Lakota interpreter was also next to a hanging strip of buffalo hide. The Parkers learned from him the many uses of buffalo outside of food, including hooves for rattles, bones for toys, hide for rope, and hair for bedding. Another interpreter was nearby showing how to scrape a hide. Morgan and James were about to partake in this when Morgan noticed the two men from the amphitheatre in the area. She watched them acting jovial, nonchalantly traipsing about the displays while apparently making jokes. Every moment or so, one of them would burst into laughter. Morgan followed them out of the corner of her eye.

Then the man with the red cap pretended to pull an imaginary bow and arrow back, and shoot a buffalo hide. "I got it!" he called out while parading around the hide.

Dad looked at the man and shook his head in disgust. "How about a little respect?" he mumbled.

Several of the native interpreters also stared at the man's antics with disbelief and disappointment.

Then the man's friend added to their charade by saying. "After we shoot it, we can just leave it to rot on the plains with the rest of the bison."

And the other replied. "And who knows, maybe those bones will eventually become fossils too."

The man with the red cap belted out a laugh and, immediately, Morgan, James, and Mom froze in unison with shivers going up their spines.

Is it Really Them?

Morgan, James, Mom, and Dad huddled together. They each took sideways, discreet glances at the two men.

Morgan was first to speak. "Is that really who I think it is?" she murmured.

"I believe so," Mom whispered back.

"Are you certain?" Dad asked. He looked over at them and whispered, "Shhh! We better keep our voices down."

The Parkers then walked around the displays, attempting to be interested in the information, but keeping a watchful, cautious eye on the potential culprits.

Finally, after a few more minutes, the suspects left the area on Native Americans and returned to the main Presidential Trail. A moment later Morgan said, "Well, what do we do now?"

Dad watched for a minute until the two men were definitely out of sight. "Are you all absolutely certain that those are the thieves?"

"Certain's a tough word," Mom mused. "I wouldn't bet my life on it, but I'll also never forget that laugh."

"I know it's the guys from Badlands who stole the bones," James blurted out. "At least I think it is."

So the Parkers decided for the time being to just continue on, hoping along the way to get a better look at them.

Abraham Lincoln

A short while later, Morgan, James, Mom, and Dad arrived at the Lincoln memorial. From there they gazed up at President Lincoln's carved face on the mountain, and quickly read over information about the sixteenth president on a plaque.

"He was president during the Civil War," Morgan realized.

"I believe you learn all about that next year in fifth grade," Mom said.

"He also delivered the Emancipation Proclamation," Dad added, "which abolished slavery in the United States."

Morgan was first to finish reading. She glanced over at the two men who were also there and whispered to her family. "It's hard to pay attention now to what we're really here for."

Then the two guys walked off. "They left," Morgan reported.

"Should we follow them?" James asked.

"What if they recognize us?" Morgan worried.

Dad thought the situation over some more. "What if all this is none of our business? After all we aren't even one hundred percent sure it's them."

After another moment at the Lincoln viewing station the family pressed on, following the prescribed route of the trail. Soon they were at the Washington memorial.

The Parkers looked directly up at President Washington. Morgan tried to take her mind off what else was going on by doing what many of the other tourists were doing, snapping photos of Washington's large stone head.

The two men were at the other end of the area, quietly talking to each other. James saw them and said, "Just seeing them makes me kind of nervous."

"You know," Dad thought out loud. "I never really saw them. All of you did. So that means, possibly, that they didn't see me," he reasoned. "And if I walk up there by myself, near them, it just might look like I'm another tourist. That way I can eavesdrop on what they're talking about. Maybe that'll help us figure out what to do."

"They're right by the Washington information sign," James whispered.

"And I want to read about Washington anyway," Dad responded. "Perhaps getting closer will give me a better idea if these really are wanted men."

Dad took a deep breath. "Well, I'm going in."

Dad took Morgan's camera. Then, nonchalantly, he meandered closer to the two men in question, and the Washington information plaque. When he got there he gazed up at the president and casually remarked. "Quite a carving up there."

The man with the red cap snickered at Dad's statement. But Dad didn't look at him. Then the man responded. "I've seen better. What nature does is more realistic, even if it takes millions of years."

Dad took a breath, digesting that comment, but

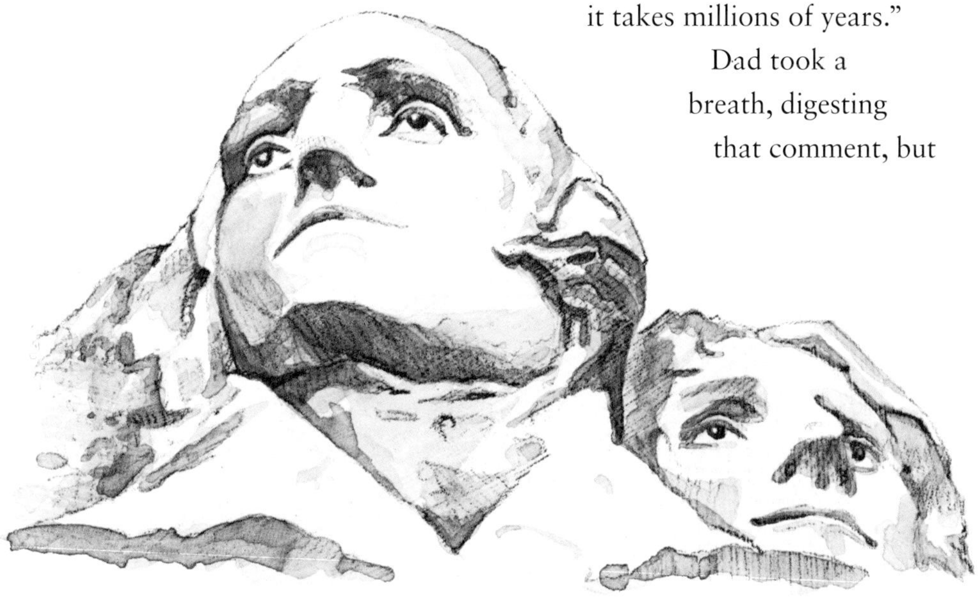

acting as if he wasn't fazed by it. Then Dad began taking photos of the mountain from various angles. Next he wandered closer to the sign, trying to focus on the information about our first president. Dad knew Washington was president between 1789 and 1797. And he was committed to democracy and the concept of "we the people," so much so that he turned down the opportunity for a third term. He didn't want to be an emperor. Dad learned that Washington played a central part in creating our constitution and that was one of the reasons he was coined "The Father of our Country."

Dad also tried to pay attention to a muted conversation going on between the two men. He inched closer, while still trying to appear most interested in the information display as well as the mountain above.

Still, Dad tuned in to the men as best he could while trying to remain discreet. With all the tourists' commotion going on around, he could only manage to hear broken bits of conversation, with things like:

"I . . . can't believe . . . much . . . found."

"Jaws . . . femur . . . skull . . ."

"Worth."

"eBay."

"Wait . . . suspicious."

At that last comment Dad couldn't help but to take a quick glance at the culprits. And they were looking right at him!

Dad swallowed nervously and looked away, while his heart began to pound. He knew he had heard enough information now. However, he waited a moment, again trying to appear to be focused elsewhere. Soon Dad walked back to his family but also noticed the two men leaving.

Once Dad was back, his family studied his transfixed, nervous gaze. "Well?" Morgan, James, and Mom's faces seemed to say.

Dad inched closer and whispered, "We have to report them to a ranger. Or the police. Or both. Now!"

The Chase Is On

The two suspects hurried down the trail, then disappeared.

Dad whispered, "What should we do?"

"We're not the police," Mom said. "It's not safe for us to be pursuing criminals."

The family looked around quickly. Although there were tons of people, there were no rangers or patrolmen in sight. So, they spent a few more minutes at the Washington memorial.

Soon they came upon the talus slope area. There, tons of granite boulders from the original carving and blasting of the mountain lay in piles of debris below the monument.

"Dynamite did most of this, I imagine," Dad mentioned, while gazing up at the slough of boulders.

The Presidential Trail

But the men weren't in sight there, so the Parkers pressed on, hoping not to get overly involved, but also hoping not to let the men get away. They spent a brief time at the Jefferson terrace stop. There they learned that because of the cracks in the rock, Jefferson's face had to be pointed upwards, as opposed to the other three presidents. But that was a unique coincidence, because that fixed his gaze out toward the plains, to the land he acquired while president, the Louisiana Purchase.

Thomas Jefferson

"That more than doubled the size of our country at the time," Mom recalled.

Soon the Parkers came to the spot they had been thinking about the most, Teddy Roosevelt. "Here's the man we've been looking for!" Dad exclaimed.

At the other end of the area were the two men.

Trying to be as inconspicuous as possible, as well as relying on the relative safety of the crowds, Morgan, James, Mom, and Dad looked up at the spectacled carving of Theodore Roosevelt, our twenty-sixth president, who held office from 1901 to 1909. They heard a person mention Roosevelt was the most controversial of the four men to be included on the memorial. But they knew one of the reasons for his inclusion was his reputation as a conservationist.

Theodore Roosevelt

"Roosevelt helped establish the national park system. More than any other president, he was the man saving national parks and monuments," Dad said, trying to muster up his usual enthusiasm.

Then Dad continued, "The Antiquities Act of 1906 was one of his big accomplishments. This allows presidents to preserve areas of land without an act of congress. Many of our famous parks were first set aside this way. And by Roosevelt! He even had his hand in saving Pinnacles—our small, but wonderful, national monument near us in California in 1908."

"I *love* Pinnacles," James whispered, while elbowing Dad in the ribs. "But they're leaving again," he gestured toward the two men.

The Parkers watched the probable bone thieves waltz down some stairs and disappear.

"Well, I don't think they think we're following them," Mom said. "At least it doesn't seem that way to me."

Morgan added. "I keep seeing a lot of the same people all along the trail. So they could easily think anyone is following them, and not us."

The Parkers started wandering over to leave when two rangers walked up. The family saw them and stopped.

"Well," Mom said. "This is our moment."

Morgan, James, Mom, and Dad walked briskly up to the rangers. "Excuse us," Dad said.

The man and woman dressed in their national park uniforms turned and looked at the Parkers. "Yes?" the woman answered.

"We'd like to report something to you," Dad replied.

"Or really, someone," Mom added. "I mean two people."

"What is it?" the man asked with growing concern.

Then all four Parkers began blurting out information.

Dad started. "We think we've spotted two bone thieves."

"They're just ahead on the trail," Mom added.

"They poached ancient mammal bones in the Badlands," James said.

"A bunch of buckets full!" Morgan added.

The Parkers kept overlapping each other while blurting out the details. Then, after a moment, the woman said, "Wait. Hold on a second. Slow down." She took a deep breath. "Are you saying, you spotted, right here on this trail, two men who took fossils illegally, last week in the Badlands?"

"That's what we're saying," Dad stated.

Then the other ranger interjected. "But in order for us to take action, we need to be certain your statements are correct. So far this is just hearsay."

Mom stepped up with more information. "When we were in the Badlands, we witnessed them putting equipment away in their car and reported it to the park rangers there."

"And I saw some of the bones," James added.

The rangers listened earnestly. "Still, that could have been a permitted dig," the woman said.

"When we reported the incident . . ." Mom started to explain further. "Wait," she interrupted herself. "I think we can prove all this." Mom fumbled through her purse until she found the scrap of paper with the car's make and the license plate of the two suspects. "I know we appear like amateur sleuths, but this is what they drove," Mom handed the paper to the rangers.

The woman looked the paper over. "A Mazda hatchback," she said, "with a South Dakota license plate."

"And you've reported this?" the man asked.

"Yep!" all four Parkers exclaimed.

"To the law enforcement personnel at Badlands," Mom added.

Then Dad asked. "Can you check to see if the car is in the parking lot?"

The woman replied, "We can. But before we get involved we have to make sure your story checks out. Also, it's an awful big parking area we have, and some of our visitors on the Fourth of July holiday park down the road and walk because of the crowds. But checking for their car is one thing we could possibly do. But first," the woman held up her cell phone.

First, she connected with dispatch on the phone and explained the situation. Then she said, "Can you verify the incident report at the Badlands from one week ago?" she glanced at the Parkers to make sure the date was correct and they nodded.

Next the woman transferred to the security personnel manning the parking garage. She spoke to them. "Do you mind sweeping the garage to look for a Mazda hatchback with a South Dakota license plate of 445 ALX. If you see that car, can you call me back right away?"

The woman put the phone down, then looked at the Parkers. "Do you mind hanging around for a little bit?"

"Not at all," Mom replied.

The two rangers and Morgan, James, Mom, and Dad stayed put at the Teddy Roosevelt memorial area. Once in a while one of them interjected some small talk into the awkward, impatient silence.

"Quite a crowd you have today," Mom said.

"Fourth of July here," the man replied. "It's our busiest of all holidays."

Morgan changed the subject. "We love it here. There's so much to learn about."

The woman looked at the Parkers and noticed they didn't have headsets. "Have you considered taking the audio tour? You can listen to a ton of information along each of the many stops on the trail."

Then the phone rang. The ranger picked it up and listened. "Go ahead. I'm here."

Morgan, James, Mom, and Dad also heard the reply. "Yes. A family of four—the Parkers—reported a bone theft incident last week. The car checks out, too. And security called us back saying there is a car that fits that description in the garage."

The two rangers looked at each other for a second. Then the woman took a step away and spoke into the phone. "We need some backup personnel to meet us along the Presidential Trail. Have them come from the end of the trail up. Right now were at the Roosevelt area. Also, please have security detain two men trying to leave in that car. And in case backup sees the suspects out here, it is two men, one tall and wearing a red ball cap."

The ranger explained a bit more of the situation to dispatch and listened to their response. Then she put down the phone and turned to the Parkers. "I think we've got to skedaddle. Please, for your own safety, let us take over from here. Thank you. You've done a good thing."

"Also," the woman added, "once this settles down, the chief ranger would like to meet with you in his office to get a few more details. Can you stop by there in an hour at the ranger station at the park entrance?"

Dad glanced at his watch. It was 6 p.m. now. "We'll be there," he replied.

And with that the two rangers took off, leaving the Parkers behind to finish the trail.

And in the End

Morgan, James, Mom, and Dad were on their own again. Each, now that things were out of their hands, seemed to take a deep breath and relax a bit.

"I'm really relieved we had a chance to report that," Mom said after several quiet moments among themselves.

"I guess we can take in the rest of the trail now until our meeting," Dad added.

The family walked on, stopping at the Sculptor's Studio a short distance later. Once there, Morgan, James, Mom, and Dad stepped inside. The room was crowded with people looking over the information. At the front a large replica of the four presidents' heads stood out among everything else on display.

"This is what they all looked at when carving the mountain, a cast replica," Dad said.

"We saw those cast replica fossils in the Badlands," Morgan recalled.

"True," Mom said. "But doesn't that seem so long ago?"

Up front several interpreters were giving demonstrations of the work and equipment used when the sculpting took place between 1927 and 1941. The Parkers stepped closer to watch.

A woman was explaining a pneumatic-powered jackhammer. "This piece of equipment," she pointed, "weighed thirty-five pounds and it was used to chip away at the rock face. Later," she added, "they used one of these." The guide gestured to another piece of machinery. "This dalette hand facer is what is called a bumping tool. It smoothed the rock surface to give the presidents more of the whitish facial complexion that we see today."

BORGLUM THE SCULPTOR

Gutzon Borglum was the American sculptor and artist who was the chief sculptor at Mount Rushmore. Trained in Paris, Borglum in his early years carved, among other things, statues for churches. But his fascination with large sculptures led him to carve an image of President Lincoln out of marble that was displayed at the Theodore Roosevelt White House. Borglum's most famous work was Mount Rushmore, which he helped originate, supervise, carve, train workers, and raise funds for the sculpture from 1927 to 1941. Unfortunately he died before the monument was completed in 1941, leaving his son Lincoln to be in charge for the finishing touches.

Borglum said of the mountain, "The purpose of the memorial is to communicate of the founding of the United States with Washington, the expansion and the Louisiana Purchase with Jefferson, the preservation of the union of the country during the Civil War with Lincoln, and development of the nation into the twentieth century with Theodore Roosevelt."

As the family watched, Morgan glanced around, and the two men were back in sight. Morgan held her breath and inched closer to her parents.

Mom caught the drift and whispered, "They're here, aren't they?"

"Yes," Morgan nodded.

Dad tried to glance discreetly about the crowded room. He glimpsed the two men across the studio. Then Dad saw the two rangers from earlier. And several other patrol personnel were nearby, appearing to be closing in.

Dad turned back to his family and reported quietly. "We're definitely not alone in here."

THIS IS THE MOUNTAIN

Harney Peak and Mount Rushmore are both located in the Black Hills and are formed of granite in a process that began 1.6 billion years ago. Later erosion exposed the granite, but it was buried again by sandstone and sediments. Then, around seventy million years ago, uplifting began thrusting up the Black Hills, which once reached twenty thousand feet above sea level. Erosion continually wore the mountains down to the four-thousand-foot or so elevation range they are today. This natural erosional process re-exposed the granite where Gutzon Borglum did his carving.

Borglum chose this mountain for several reasons: 1) It is made of a smooth, fine-grained granite. 2) The granite was durable and erosion-resistant. 3) It is the tallest mountain in the region. 4) The mountain faces the southeast so workers got maximum sunlight exposure when carving the mountain and the sculpture.

The Parkers tried to focus on the interpreter's presentation as she continued talking about the smoothing process. But that proved to be difficult as their minds were elsewhere. Then, some commotion in the back interrupted everything.

"Let's get out of here," the man in the red cap called to his buddy. The two took off jogging. And, quickly, all uniformed patrol were in full pursuit.

Morgan saw the chase just as they left the area. "We were right in the middle of the action!" she exclaimed.

"Now we can be certain those are the guys," Mom said. "Or else why would they be running?"

After the law enforcement officers took off after the criminals, the Parkers also left the studio. They climbed some stairs to a viewing terrace. "I wonder what's going to happen," James said.

"Well, I just hope they catch them and the fossils are returned," Dad added.

At the terrace the family saw a group of people with headsets, using the audio tour. One person there said to her companions, "Did you hear what they just said on this?"

And she quoted Borglum from the device. "Do you see those faces? They're in there. All I have to do is bring them out from under all that rock."

Those words grabbed the Parkers' attention.

"The faces were already in the rock," Dad echoed. "All the sculptor had to do was bring them out."

"Hmm," Dad pondered further. "Seems like this was the perfect place for this monument. The granite was all set and ready to be carved and chiseled."

Finally, the Parkers left the Presidential Trail altogether. With some time still remaining before their meeting, they went to get a quick bite to eat at the cafeteria. While they were paying for their food, a man in uniform walked up to them.

"Excuse me," he said "are you the Parkers?"

"Yes," Dad replied.

"I'm Navnit Singh, the chief ranger here at Mount Rushmore. Do you mind if I ask you a few questions?"

"You were the person we were going to meet?" Mom asked.

"Yep."

"How did you find us?" Dad asked.

"You match your description perfectly."

With that Morgan, James, Mom, and Dad took their food to a table, accompanied by Ranger Singh.

Mom introduced everyone in her family. From there the chief ranger wanted to hear the whole story about the poached bones from the beginning. The Parkers filled him in on all the details they could remember from almost a week ago on the Castle Trail, until the events of today. Finally when they appeared to be done, Mr. Singh asked, "Have you left anything out?"

"I don't think so," Dad replied. He glanced at his family but they all shrugged their shoulders indicating that was all they knew.

"Well," Mr. Singh replied. "I've got some news for all of you."

The Parkers sat forward in anticipation.

"First of all," the chief ranger began, "we did apprehend those two men. It was quite a ruckus when we managed to corner them in the parking lot. But, thankfully, it ended peacefully and no one was hurt. We were also able to search their car. Would you believe the fossils, buckets, tools, and all were still in there?"

"Anyway," the chief ranger went on, "we have since made a few calls to the folks at the Badlands, including their chief paleontologist, Rachel Benton. Incidentally, she spoke quite highly of all of you." Mr. Singh smiled at the Parkers. "We described what we recovered and she was extremely relieved and thankful. And," he added, "Ms. Benton has a personal message for you folks."

Mr. Singh took out an official-looking piece of paper, put on some reading glasses, and looked at Morgan, James, Mom, and Dad. "She just e-mailed this to me. Are you all ready?"

The Parkers nodded enthusiastically.

"Dear Morgan, James, Robert, and Kristen Parker," the ranger began, "Thank you so much for helping us recover the stolen fossils from the Badlands. You don't know how important that is to us. The park and the scientific world are certainly a much better place for this."

The amazing Black Hills

"Furthermore," the Chief Ranger read while glancing up at four beaming faces, "that fossil bed you discovered along the Castle Trail is proving to be quite a find. We've now done a preliminary survey of the site and that afternoon we were able to identify a saber-toothed cat skull that appears articulated, which is extremely rare. And it looks like the whole area is full of many, many more bones. So far we've seen some teeth, parts of a jaw, vertebra pieces, a leg bone, and more of a skull that we'll need to dig out. Some of the bones of different animals were very close to each other, specifically that of a *Mesohippus* and the saber-toothed cat. We may have ourselves another Pig Dig. Many of the fossils are so intermingled, we think they may have died at the same time, and that could also help explain the scar on the *Mesohippus* jaw you saw.

"Welcome to paleontology. It is such a fascinating field! And what you found for us is a display of a unique preservation of animals from more than thirty million years ago. It will help us learn about their whole ecosystem and the predator-prey relationships they had going on. My best guess is the area was one of the very last watering holes around during an extended drought.

"It also looks like we're going to be there for quite some time. If we get funding grants, the dig may last several years or perhaps longer. We are just getting initial plans together for that now.

"So, if ever you are in the area again, please stop by and say hello, and then come join us out at the dig that *you all started*." Mr. Singh showed the family that Rachel had highlighted those words. "If you can't find it, this time we'll show you the way! With much gratitude, Rachel Benton, Chief Paleontologist, Badlands National Park."

Chief Ranger Singh folded the e-mail and handed it to Mom. "It looks like you are making quite a name for yourselves out in this neck of the woods," he said. Then the director stood up and shook each of the Parkers' hands.

"Oh, one more thing," he said, pulling out another piece of paper. "This document entitles each of you to a free audio tour, whenever you want to use it."

Morgan smiled. "Thanks! That was actually our plan for tomorrow."

"Perfect," Mr. Singh replied. Then he said good-bye to the family.

Amphitheatre at Mount Rushmore

Meanwhile, Morgan, James, Mom, and Dad skedaddled over to the amphitheatre. They sat there with much anticipation watching people gather for the traditional evening lighting ceremony. As the time drew nearer, Morgan and James concurred on a top ten list for their trip in James's journal:

1. Severe storms and storm chasers in the Badlands
2. Notch Trail and ladder and bighorn sheep at Badlands
3. Prairie Dog Town in the Badlands
4. The Castle Trail at the Badlands (and going up Saddle Pass)
5. Bison herd at Wind Cave
6. Wind Cave Candlelight Tour
7. Natural Entrance Tour—Wind Cave
8. Mount Rushmore Presidential Trail
9. Finding a bunch of fossil mammals and helping catch the bone thieves at Mount Rushmore
10. The lighting of the presidents' heads! (Which is just about to start.)

Good-bye until next time,

Morgan and James Parker